The Ungrateful

The Ungrateful

Ramesh Pokhriyal 'Nishank'

Published by
PRABHAT PRAKASHAN PVT. LTD.
4/19 Asaf Ali Road,
New Delhi-110 002 (INDIA)
e-mail: prabhatbooks@gmail.com

ISBN 978-93-90923-77-9
THE UNGRATEFUL
novel by Shri Ramesh Pokhriyal 'Nishank'

Edition
First, 2021

Price
₹ 350.00 (Rupees Three Hundred Fifty only)

Printed at
R-Tech Offset Printers, Delhi

One

It was a cool winter morning. The winter chill pierced through the veins and interdicted us from physically popping out of our warm and cozy comforts. Some of us resolved frequently to resume our morning walks but with every coming morning, due to the chill, we would be inept to summon up about what we had resolved and would tightly clutch our quilts and prefer to remain inside. However, there had been some passionate enthusiasts, whom nothing could stop from leaving their homes, despite the severe wintery chill. Among them were people of all ages, children, young and the old ones, whom we could see, albeit much less in number in the winter, exercising and jogging around in the colonies parks. Their early morning appearance in parks gave an impression that, maybe, it was not the time of cool winter winds blowing everywhere.

Ambuj firmly maintained his routine of leaving his bed quite early at five every morning, dressing up himself in his morning-walk attire and reaching the colony park, for few minutes jog followed by half an hour exercise and return home. Everyone in his family and friend circle would call Ambuj a 'fitness freak'.

However, on one recent morning, Ambuj kept sleeping until half past six and did not wake up as per his schedule. His wife, Varsha gently nudged him to wake up and kept a cup of tea on the bedside table. Ambuj popped out his face from the cozy quilt and glanced through the clock.

"Why haven't you nudged me up? How late it is today?" "Why should I wake you up? It was almost two o'clock last night when you went to bed. This much sleep is essential to remain healthy," Varsha replied with a smile. "But you have slept only after my arrival. Is sleep not required for your better health?" Ambuj asked his wife.

"I stay at home all the day. I can rest anytime in the day but you will leave for work now and I am not sure about when you would return," she intonated in an indistinct accent of remonstration and handed over the cup of tea to Ambuj.

Ambuj was the only son of Ramnathji, a reputed businessperson, and Varsha was his wife. Despite the whole train of servants in the house, Varsha had maintained one rule for many years, to serve the morning tea to Ambuj with her own hands. No matter how hectic the routine was, the mornings for Ambuj always commenced with the comforting presence of Varsha. Throughout the day, Ambuj would not get leisure time from his work. He would often hastily gulp the day's meal in the office, and sometimes he would not even get even that time for lunch. Naturally, Varsha would definitely wait for him for their dinner tim, to be together, Ambuj was conscious of Varsha's precept, thus, he would never skip to inform his wife whenever he would be late.

"Newspaper, please" he asked his wife.

"Have your tea first. Do not waste your time by browsing through the news headlines."

"May I know why you were late?" Varsha asked. "I don't know anything," replied Ambuj. Varsha left to return with the newspaper.

Ambuj had two elder sisters, who were happy in their matrimonial residences. Ambuj's father, grandfather and great grandfather were property owners of this region. They were, in fact, feudal lords of the province. As India had gained freedom, princely provinces were annexed to the Indian state. Even the kings of that era, too, surrendered their lands and contemplated to espouse another profession. Anyway, who does not change, according to the dictates of the time? Ramnathji, thus, launched his own business. He became the proprietor of the sole agency of Ambassador cars in the encompassing area. Gradually, he proceeded to expand the business further and hitherto, he owned the agency of numerous big and small Indian and foreign vehicles.

Despite protest from his wife, Ramnathji had secured Ambuj admission in a prestigious boarding school. Ambuj was an innocent boy until but then he witnessed disparity among human beings for the first time.

The institutional charges of the boarding school were so enormous that children of average families could not afford to study there. Yet, children from these affluent schools were sometimes taken to the slums to make them learn the concept of social enterprises. Sometimes, these wealthy kids would teach kids of the poor. More than others, Ambuj felt inspired to engage in this exercise. He would get mentally perturbed to discern the pathetic condition of these children. Ambuj would frequently donate something of his own to these poor children, while returning.

"Papa, God has created us all, isn't it?"

Ambuj asked his father when he arrived back home during the vacations and his father nodded in affirmation. Ramnathji would often wonder how Ambuj at his tender age would think so big.

"Then why is someone so poor and the other so rich?"

The repeated queries of innocent Ambuj would often

make his father speechless. Because Ambuj wanted an explanation, Ramnathji would just calm down the curiosity of his son. Hence, he conveniently associated the economic incongruence of the poor with lesser efforts made by them. "Son, those who work hard become rich and those who sit indolently endure poverty," Ramnathji would say.

Ambuj was unconvinced by his father's haggard rejoinder and retorted, "But Papa, those people work harder than us. They break stones; they work for wages, why are they deprived still?"

Ramnath was startled to confront the response from his son. How deeply can this little child assume? Now, how should he elucidate? Indeed, any additional clarification was not deemed appropriate for the child and Ramnathji deferred saying anything further.

The simple perception of the child Ambuj could not understand this theory of poverty and wealth. He strived to ascertain an explanation to this enigma but could never grasp one.

This concern intensified in the mind of naive Ambuj. Whenever he saw helpless and needy people, he was sensitive enough to feel disturbed. Ramnath accepted that as Ambuj would grow up in years, his perception would further widen, and this would be extricated from his subconscious.

Ramnathji had pinned a colossal expectation from Ambuj to manage his business and expand it after finishing his education. However, observing these inclinations of the son, he could grasp that his expectations from Ambuj for developing his business were becoming shallow.

After the termination of the princely rule of the states, he had managed to maintain his status. On the contrary, many princely states had been wiped out due to their indolence and incompetence. Owing to his intellect and foresightedness, he never suffered any monetary loss. However, he had started feeling that his son would obliterate his well-established business due to his ideology. Unaware of the business's norms and oblivious of the class differences, Ambuj possessed a sympathetic demeanor towards the poor. Ramnathji decoded to keep Ambuj away from this environment. As soon as he passed out of school, he was sent abroad for his graduation.

Ambuj's departure to a foreign land posthaste made him to conjecture his father's intentions, for he was no longer a kid. His father's decision to send him away from this environment was not underestimated either. No capitalist father would ever appreciate attraction of his only son towards socialism. Ramnathji, too, enjoyed realizing social responsibilities like all those who belonged to the business community. He conceded to his business establishment's social responsibilities and held the position of president of several charitable institutions located in the city. He had been bestowing considerable endowments to various social events.

Nevertheless, it was also a part of his business management. Owing to his business committals, he would get many occasions to congregate with prominent people and influential politicians. These meetings would provide him another reservoir of opportunities for his business.

After sending Ambuj away to study about business management in a far-flung foreign land, Ramnathji was sure that a change of thought would emerge. If he would be hypnotized by America's vivid life, he would understand everything and would concede to his own initiatives. Ramnathji was sure of the changes in Ambuj after returning from America that he would manage the business on his own accord.

□

Two

Time passed very fast. Meanwhile, as he was prudent of his eminence, social ethics and society's norms, Ramnathji married away both his daughters. He had an evident zeal to arrange the marriage and sacraments of both his daughters according to his social standing and prestige. Meanwhile, Ambuj would visit his parents in between whenever he had vacations. He had startlingly become silent on that childhood ambivalence with which he always nettled his father. He speculated that his father had sent him to a far-flung area across seven seas to keep him away at a distance from everything.

Five years later, after completing his MBA course from a prestigious institution in the US, Ambuj returned to follow the family business. Ramnathji was elated to receive his son with the revived discernment that Ambuj would join hands with him for their family business and tread along like a business acquaintance. Ambuj could clearly visualize how the community has evolved and how gender-norms were still visible, which included apparent gaps in redemptive satisfaction when it came to involve his parents. He was mesmerized to see the most straightforward joy in his mother, for whom the physically evident presence of her only son was a rich source of ocular jubilation. His mother had questioned her husband when he had decided to pass the tough verdict of sending Ambuj abroad for his further studies.

"Are there no good colleges in India? Does he really need to do a job? After all, he has to manage your business." "Janaki, there are good colleges in India, and Ambuj will manage to get admission in those colleges, but I see that his focus is more towards doing social service than pursuing his studies. First, he has to complete his education, and then he can do whatever he wishes to. Hence, it is necessary to send him out at this juncture," asked Ambuj's mother.

The sentiments of Ambuj's mother were smothered within the four walls of the house. She was not even allowed to cry, while her son was getting ready to leave. She bottled-up all her tears and her lamentations within her. Sometimes Janaki would be frustrated but would remain calm to present a pseudo-appearance of the noble gentry. Wasn't she a human being?

Janaki somehow endured her grief, her suffering and her anguish with recalcitrant fortitude, and spent five years waiting for him. When Ambuj visited home during the holidays, either once a year or after six months, Janaki would yearn with an aching heart to see him. Lastly, she was happy that after an extended interim, her waiting time was over. Notwithstanding his resilience, Ambuj would sometimes become pensive and would fondly remember his mother. He felt more connected to her than he would towards his father. Even during his stay in America, he would talk to his mother more. Janaki was even more isolated especially after the marriage of her daughters. She felt passed-over, neglected and isolated in a big bungalow. Her husband would be diligently engaged with his business commitments, while she would be languishing solely at home.

"I will also accompany you to Delhi to receive Ambuj," Janaki pleaded with her husband, to which he readily agreed.

Surajpur was only a four-hour drive from Delhi yet, these four hours emerged vexatious to Janki. She consciously immersed herself in the nostalgic recollection of Ambuj's childhood to consume time.

When they reached Delhi, the airport's wait was longer than expected that shattered Janaki's patience. Repeatedly, she nagged her husband about the timings of Ambuj's flight, while Ramnath smiled at her innocent restlessness.

"Why are you precipitous? The flight will come, and I am his father and not his foe. I am also abiding by the timings."

"You had not kept him for nine months in your womb?" said Janki with wet eyes.

"What a funny statement by the mother! By keeping the child for nine months in the womb, you understand that no one can love the child more than the mother can. You women behave as if fathers had never been there." Ramnath was trying to recreate his wife's impatient understanding.

Finally, Ambuj's flight landed. Janaki's eyes were glued to the exit door of the airport from where the passengers were pouring out. When Ambuj emerged in sight into his mother's longing eyes, he caught the sight of his mother. Emotional Janki grabbed him closer to her heart as he approached her from nigh.

The trio—father-son-mother—continued chatting incessantly all along the way from the airport to Surajpur. The journey of four hours that had appeared a long journey to Janki while proceeding to the airport from Surajpur, the same appeared incredibly shorter to her while driving back on the same route. Human action transcends the vast expanse of expectations. Everyone owned his own peculiar discernment for the exhilaration of arriving home. Ramnathji was happy that Ambuj, his young and professionally proficient son, the family descendant, would now share his business burden and support him. At the same time, Janaki was happy for the most straightforward logic that her son would be amidst the family and more so around her.

It took more than a fortnight for Ambuj to reconcile to the new surroundings and the armored expectations from him. Before Ramnathji could say something, Ambuj had started going to the office with him. Ramnath was pleased. Everything surfaced on the scenario precisely as what he had anticipated. Ambuj followed a peculiar way of proceeding with the official matters; remained cognizant of everything, of every precise specification and details possessed narrow details of everything from accounts to employees. He would gather an erudite information about business functioning and transcribe it.

In a fleeting interim period, Ambuj accomplished excellent heights in his father's business. Ramnathji possessed a coveted desires that his son Ambuj should implement the management proficiencies that he had studied in his degree course to expand his business further. Scattered deep within, Ramnathji suffered mystical trepidation, as any father does, and the cynical skepticism constantly nagged him about what could be transpiring within the subterranean crypts in Ambuj's sub-consciousness and what were his inclinations. Yes, it was subterranean! Ramnathji failed to estimate Ambuj's real propensities.

Moreover, after dinner one night, he managed an opportune moment to convene with Ambuj.

"Son! What do you think about it now?" Ramnathji asked.

"A lot. Many things are raging in my mind. There are many plans for the future," replied Ambuj.

Noticing the luminosity of hope in Ambuj's eyes, Ramnathji was sanguine about the fulfillment of his dreams. He conjectured that the rage of time has thrown the demon off Ambuj's crest. He concluded that many years of the academic exodus to the alien land might have transformed him into an effective revisionist. Still, when he heard Ambuj's convictions and beliefs, then he recognized that he was highly mistaken in assessing Ambuj. He had failed to understand his young mind. Ambuj initiated his talk with the blueprint; Ramnathji was shocked and felt the ground had slipped from under his feet.

"Dad, our business is performing admirably and would continue to advance in the future as well, but at the social level, we have not been able to ensure our presence on the social platform."

"But son, I am Chairman and a mentor of many social and religious institutions." Ramnathji asserted while being sagacious about what Ambuj said and what he meant by it, as if any other parent nourished an unarticulated, implicit nervousness of being opposed.

"No, dad, I don't mean that." Ambuj was resolute since he fondled the obligation of social accountability towards the impoverished.

"Then what do you mean, what do you want?"

"Yeah, something concrete for the benefit of some real, afflicted, and vulnerable person." Sighing, Ambuj propped back on the chair. The predictable idea of social work made him smile, while he speculated to focus on his mission. He greeted the ensuing reticence.

"Like?" Ramnathji squealed in exasperation, while sustaining the low amplitude in his voice as he already lived apprehending this.

"The *ashrams* for widows and destitute women,

refugees homes for orphans, reasonably good schools for them, and so on."

"Oh, is that so! The phantasm of social service has not yet plunged down from your mind." Ramnathji said in exasperation with the puff of wind from his rounded lips as he plunged into deliberation. He felt as if his illusionary bastion of mammoth enterprise that he had fondly upstretched for over so many years appeared to be on the verge of collapse. Ambuj read and evidently noticed the facial expressions of his father.

"Dad, I will not let this affect my business, But just think the peace of my mind that I will receive by helping someone in need." Ambuj was aware of his father's passion for his business establishment and assured him where he felt it would sway his father the most. His raspy and gritty voice cut through the air.

"But son, we keep doing charitable work. Our ancestors have been helping not only the helpless and the poor, but also," Ramnathji argued performing a series of mental calculations. His mind coiled around his target consequentially expended most of his time in negotiations and corporate partnerships.

"No, not that, father, it is just that I want our undeviating involvement in the dome of social service," Ambuj retorted the squabble rationally. Ramnathji preferred to say nothing to his son, or rather; he purposely wished to evade the tiff.

There was silence in the room for some time. Both Ramnathji and Ambuj were engrossed in their respective thoughts. While Ramnathji was deeply engrossed in doing many calculations, computing strategic possibilities with the hope of putting together his blueprint schemata, Ambuj was engaged in providing concrete shape to his passion. Ramnathji's mind remained beleaguered in summoning up the recollections from the bygone days encouraging sadness within followed by silent declarations. He ruminated on the efforts of his regal ancestors, who owned the entire region. Times changed, circumstances changed. The kingly states were annexed to the Indian republic.

Industrious, hardworking, and respectable Ramnathji, with the forte of his mental acumen, had fortified a topnotch industrialist position in Surajpur and the surrounding industrial world and wished to scale new heights for his enterprise.

Ramnathji, coaxed by lavishness, abundance, affluence, and the rich annals of family history coveted for an administrative position, twice pondered about contesting the elections but later changed his plan. He somehow relegated his desire to the background to send his son Ambuj abroad for higher education. Ramnathji was absorbed in his fostered desires but later hinged on Ambuj to fetch those yearnings to full rotation.

While Ramnathji wished to be reputable as a leading industrialist in his area, Ambuj proceeded the other way. When he was younger, he could be understood for his passions, and he could be easily turned to the ways of his father. After Ambuj had secured his MBA degree from the prestigious institute abroad, he was not short of work, for big industrial houses were waiting in the wings to chartering an impressive job figuration for him on a thick handsome package. Ramnathji, who wished his son to cooperate with him in his business after procuring his esteemed degree from abroad, pondered that if he would go against him, he would refuse him and would even set off against his bidding. The idea that he was capable of forsaking even his father, shook Ramnathji out of his mind when he contemplated that even the slightest opposition to Ambuj's plan would make him renounce his business and who knew that he might have started a new job as well. After all, his gargantuan passion had been more significant than the rest. Then what would have been left for Ramnathji? Ambuj was his only one son, and ultimately everything belonged to him. Ramnathji kept churning the possibilities within and, in conclusion, resolved to twirl with laying down the arms and forfeit his imaginings for a moment.

"What do you think, father?" Ambuj's question shook listless Ramnathji out of his torpor. Ramnathji had mentally calculated all the profits and losses, had apprised Ambuj of his rejoinder, while he maintained an unruffled and somber expression. "Son, I'm old now. Your assessments are innovative, and you possess a renewed dynamism. Without hesitation, if you accomplish the business however, you would prefer, I am good with it. Do as you deem fit." While articulating his viewpoint, a kind of tumultuous waves emerged within him that even a superciliously educated boy like Ambuj could not fathom.

Experience outstripped modern education, which is like the fresh cogitations but indeed not as wise. Ambuj, with significant and violent desires with and without perturbations that had not been ripe for his age, believed that his father had voluntarily tendered over the business to him, felt exultant at this transpiration. The fiery passion that fulminated within him had been fuelled and invigorated, making him demonstrative.

"Dad, don't say that. You will always be an inspiration, and I will always need your immense experiences." Ambuj touched Ramnath's feet to seek his blessings with an upsurge of emotional crescendo. Ramnath hugged him.

Ramnathji was expressively soothed within for devouring a fresh sparkling wave and invigorating ecstasy.

That day, Ramnathji, with his power of understanding, comprehended one thing had though he repudiated his son; wherefore, he stumbled across the contentment that he had grasped while nestling him in his arms. His soul was illuminated with the echo of the luminosity that emerged from Ambuj's eyes. He fathomed that the current account balance of that moment was considerably higher and more treasurable than the entire incremented gross revenue turnover from his business. Moreover, Ramnathji experienced an indeterminate emotional encumbrance debark from psyche. That night, both Ambuj and Ramnathji, slept peacefully and mesmerized.

After procuring the unswerving acquiescence from the father, Ambuj commenced in full swing, like an eager beaver, towards the actualization of his dreams with a clean slate.

The father was convinced that his son now has a life course to follow, but Janki was not assured. In fact, the mother, under no circumstances, hankers after any moments of relaxation, especially with her children. It has been that way; the mother was—paranoid and obsessed.

Janki nourished auxiliary strategies mysteriously hidden under her sleeves. She longed for more, dreamt more, and cared more. There was contentment that had loomed large for Janaki when she glimpsed her son had returned home. She appreciated him that he had assimilated himself in his father's business. However, straight away, it was her prospect for the actualization of her imaginings regarding procuring conjugal happiness for his son. She envisaged getting a decent bride for Ambuj, a girl who would be his significant other, which Janki wished to realize almost immediately, a yearning that she had already articulated to her son.

"Mother, wait only for two years. Then do what you want."

That was an excellent surmise for the mother. Anyways, it would have taken some time for her to stumble upon the desirable prospective girl as a bride for him; hence, she decided to kick off exploring for her from the succeeding year.

□

Three

A devouring span of two years had elapsed expeditiously. Meanwhile, Ambuj was industriously occupied with his family enterprise and that had instantaneously hounded his passions. Janaki had been fondling with her get-up-and-go enterprise to determine an appropriate partner for her son.

Unambiguously, Ambuj was oblivious of his mother's concerns for his conjugal alliance. He had been busy constructing care centers for the helpless and destitute womenfolk on his land that had been lying vacant for years and created employment projections for them under the same roof. Harmonizing the economic equivalence between the rich and the impoverished was the sole motto of his life. He made strategies, coordinated with self-help groups, arranged for monetary support from the governmental organizations, and spoke with the agencies for the skilled for extending training programs to these women supported by him. Ambuj ensured to make these women proficient in the artisanship of sewing, embroidery, weaving, pickle, and papad-making for self-sustenance. Consequentially, he supplied them with raw materials for accomplishing their artisanship. Ambuj constructed a school for the underprivileged, impoverished, and deprived children and employed trained teachers to make these children equivalent to the rest. Ambuj had acquired knowledge, awareness, and familiarity, while pursuing his management degree; he poured that knowledge into accomplishing his vision.

Nonetheless, Ambuj remained wrapped up around his worktop for formulating strategies, while his mind kept swimming for more ideas. Nevertheless, nothing was gratifying to him than the progress of his work, which projected to the surface like never anticipated, for which he had burnt the midnight oil and shattered all his mental, physical and emotional energies. He remained unmindful of the anxieties curdling inside his stomach, resentful of his choice aggrieved by any surmounting, simultaneously, actualizing his project into reality, a project for which he had willingly renounced his moments of relaxation. It was then; Varsha entered his life, bringing fresh air like in a bucolic surroundings.

When Janki's choice initially bumped into Varsha that was almost after one and a half years of bride hunting for her well-deserved son she instantaneously and intuitively comprehended that she could be the perfect match for Ambuj and can systematize his life accordingly. Relying on her experiences, she further spearheaded the matter of the matrimonial alliance. Any objections from Varsha's parents were unquestionable, for anyways, what objections could they raise. Since there were no objections, the matrimonial relationship between the two was fixed with both the families' mutual consent. Varsha belonged to a respectable but reasonably prosperous family.

The buoyancy of her contentment resonated through Janki's conviction that Varsha, bestowed to spend her life with Ambuj, appeared gorgeous, soft-spoken, and cultured. Additionally, her presumptions were not erroneous.

Varsha entered into Ambuj's life, justifying the ancient adage that followed the proverb of 'Like Name, Same Quality' like the advent of the cool breezy spray in the scorching summer heat. Before Varsha's arrival, Ambuj felt being in manacles and inertly blamed his mother for manipulating the forceful and unauthorized intrusion of a mystically unknown person into his life. Varsha, conversely slipped into the family fold with Ambuj, and her doting parents-in-law, slowly and steadily made an impressive family and became their beloved.

Until Ambuj entered into conjugal bliss with Varsha, he would persistently remain too occupied with his passion for social service and never consciously made an effort to reach home in time. All these rehabilitated after the onset of Varsha into his life, and all of his erstwhile schedules rescinded. Now, Ambuj always looked forward to a rationalization to come home timely, while Varsha too would not eat food until he reached home and kept herself occupied in the house's day-to-day happenings.

Unbranded and unclaimed elusive time stops for none. The time sallied forth with tranquility and delightfully. The works established by Ambuj had moved towards its prosperity. He had found his reputation large and wide in social work that he could interfere in many social organizations running in and around the city. He liked to work more in profundity than superficial. He had given shelter to many children and had linked many destitute women to self-employment.

Meanwhile, he had become the father of two daughters. Ramnathji was contented with the evolution of his son's commercial perspicacity, and the seizure that his son would ruin his business was no more gnawing at him. Ambuj would take the business guidance from his father on every significant and insignificant matter. He grappled with the aspiration to do something for his parents' cheerfulness had now been predominant in his list of priorities.

"Father, if you want to contest elections, contest it now.

Now you will also get the votes of the poor", when Ambuj pronounced this to his father, it was applauded with elation as his son's spiritual evolution and his consternations emanating from his awareness of his shallow knowledge in the past, and his growing sobriety.

"How correct was his son. When he thought of contesting elections, he was whirling under the influence of his wealth and was flummoxed with it. He had arrogantly desired to secure the political ticket to power riding atop his economic status and contesting elections. Simultaneously, he possessed a conviction that his affluent friends would support him to emerge victorious in those elections. However, how wrong were they? It was good that he did not commit that mistake. Otherwise, his conceited comprehension would have scattered both his pride and honor."

Ramnathji was resolved to his providence with great strength of feeling, the composure of temper and cheerfulness of manner, and did not suckle any such aspiration. Now, what concerned him the most was his son's progress, and receiving the affection of the people and the blessings of the poor and the needy that there was no scope left for any other happiness? The climax of mental pleasure emerged from watching Ambuj and his rich associations with social concerns of essential parameters and had to wrestle with discrete people. The course of social service had never been contented for Ambuj, for he had to grapple with the legal hassle and sometimes even with the police. Most horrendously, one such incident had taken place the previous night, which became the prominent reason for Ambuj's late arrival; moreover, he wished to read about that incident in the tabloid. How congruous had been the whole incident, what could be the truth that Ambuj suffered the head-splitting tumult, was not even aware of, so he desired to comprehend the real and how the incident had been projected in the newspapers was his primary concern.

Varsha brought the whole bunch of newspapers and placed them in front of Ambuj. Ambuj kept the national newspaper sideways and seized upon the local newspaper.

'A woman unsuccessful has consumed poison.'

'Unhappy maiden gulped down poison because of aunt's torture.'

Similar headings occurred in different newspapers. Ambuj read the story further. He wanted to gauge the news' authenticity from most news articles but strongly suspected the twisted tale for augmenting its sales. However, the name of the girl had been replaced with a fictitious name to maintain her secrecy. 'At least, the over-enthusiastic journalists had taken care of this.'

Ambuj was very irritated with the journalists howling unpleasant accusations with bizarre deliberate inventions without mulling over the personal life, self-respect, and impact on the person's future. However, these newspapers still published frolicsome newsflash to bourgeon the sales of their newspaper by making it appear piquant and peppery.

There were scores of girls and women in his care center, who suffered numerous glitches and provocations, which is one aspect of their personal life, which had been very excruciating and never did they wish their personal matters to be made public. Ambuj coveted to do everything possible to protect them from those journalists, who were embroiled in sordid contretemps. It could be achieved because of his active involvement with social work and his good relations with the city's eminent journalists. They also supported him in this noble cause but then there was no shortage of those with earnest endeavors to make journalism their business.

He still could not erase the face of the girl from his memory, a girl who had lost her life due to glitches and provocative news coverage by journalists. The eighteen-year-old teenager, angry with her mother, left the house and went to a friend's house, who lived in rented accommodation with two or three other girls. The parents kept searching for their daughter but did not report the matter to the police for fear of social slander.

The desperate search for four to five days with all relatives and friends could not fetch them any positive response. The entire week passed by, but later they discovered her in jail for the offense of prostitution. Those girls introduced her to a woman, advertently known as an aunt; the unscrupulous aunt introduced her to her customers. She spluttered, tried to run but could not be successful.

Her dreaded fate to suffer all that was not meant to sustain for a longer time. When one day, the police raided the premises of her refuge, she was caught. The influential people secured her bail but there was none to listen to her side of the story. Owing to social ignominy, she could not even tell them the names of her parents and their addresses.

When the calamity suffered by this girl became evident, she was brought to Ambuj's care center and was provided shelter there. When she entered the center, her mental state was despondent, and she would find refuge in incessant howling and crying, screaming all the time, and cry aloud. It was a case of rape, not of a body trade, which mauled her body, and more than the body, her soul was mangled. One of those days, one of the wicked photographers published her story with her photograph and name. Devastated by the news article's publication, revealing the victim's picture with a name to the world, her parents arrived in the newspaper's office with a piece of newspaper in their hand. The unfortunate but guileless and unassuming parents of the victim were not cognizant of the world's pseudo diktats and had a near negligible grasp of the veracity that they had mentioned when they arrived, they could be said to have been already delayed by then. God knows from where the girl had predetermined the horrid step and had prearranged a bottle of liquefied oil and a matchbox. Probably death appeared more tranquil to her than to stay alive. In an appalling incident, to avoid any latitude for subsistence, the girl had ripped-open the nerves of her wrist before setting herself on fire.

When the parents reached there, they discovered how despicable their situation was and how horrendously their daughter's burnt body was lying there in front of them. More than anything, the most penetrating had been the heart- wrenching note from their ill-fated daughter had awaited them. "Now everyone would know, how will my parents appear before the people with so much ignominy and how my parents will tolerate so much slander, it is better that I die." It would be appropriate to call it an open daylight murder instead of suicide, but who could be held responsible for this ghastly act. Was the girl, who left her home in her displeasure, responsible? On the other hand, were her fraudulent friends who handed her to Aunty, responsible? Or was it that crooked and deceitful Aunty who commandeered away the whole kit and caboodle from her? For fear of public mortification and calumny, the parents did not testify the matter even to the police.

Had not the whole world chipped into the incident! Everyone partakes in the responsibility for this, everyone possessed an elfin commitment, but the blunder that had been committed could have been effortlessly revamped. Undeniably, the abrasion was abysmally profound, but could it not be nurtured with unguents and ointments. Public memory is short. Gradually, the people would have quickly forgotten the incident. Still, that news published in the tabloid had broken her patience when she decided her onward journey into the next world, where there was no one to recognize her, where none would have known her pain, where none would have slandered her.

Ambuj could never exonerate that journalist for the defamatory news article. What is the news of such actuality, which filches the existence of a human being?

It is mentioned in the *Manusmriti*, "One should state what is true, and one should state what is pleasing. One should refrain from stating the unpleasant truth and refrain from stating what is pleasant even if it is false."

Years ago, our ancestors tried to make us understand this dictum through the verse.

Ambuj's organization appropriated a breather the instant they had efficaciously hauled the editors of that publication to the witness box, they wrestled the case prompted by and taking the cue from that scandalous news article, against the tabloid in the court to set an example and present an ethical model for the others in the future. Ambuj was resolute, Ambuj was agitated and Ambuj had annexed an earnest expletive on his conscience, for he was bound by an oath to not rest until the detractors are booked in the court of justice. He resolved to ensure that none in the future could take the liberty of slanging the other's reputation, and none procures the right to play with someone's life under the sticky label of truth.

Ambuj started reviewing the case further. Some

newspapers articulated their unconfirmed story of the girl eating poison after being deceived in love. They too confirmed the news in an affirmative tone; others had established the bewitched aunt's narrative and put the onus of the girl's death on her aunt's sorcery. Initially, Ambuj did not possess many tidings about the entire fatal incident. In spite of everything, when the girl was rushed to the hospital after she had consumed poison, Ambuj was present there, engrossed in some vital conversation with the chief medical officer when the police inspector arrived and informed the medical officer about the occurrence.

Her uncle had brought the girl in an unconscious state to the hospital, while her aunt stood there petrified. She regained now conscious but was not in a condition to talk. There was already a colossal gathering of bystanders, with as many stories fabricated, trickled down and propagated. Ironically, every person at the hospital gate wished to know more about the whole incident, what might have conspired? Who could be held responsible? Was it suicide or murder? While her uncle stood with his head stooped down, and back hunched and her aunt repeatedly reiterated her unwillingness to take her home with them.

"She has defamed the entire family, will get us imprisoned one day. Who will look after my children after that?" Then, she started howling and beating her chest simultaneously.

The girl remained quiet when the police wished to record her official statement after she regained consciousness. She refrained from impugning any person even though repeatedly investigated and prodded for the answers. She repeated once or twice that she did not wish to survive and had lost her fascination for life.

Ambuj requested police officers to wait for a day or two

to further investigate and record her official statements. By then, her mental state would have also recovered, and she would be mentally in a position to account for the raison d'être for the perversity of her suicide attempt.

Police returned at Ambuj's behest, while he accessed the medical team attending to her condition. She was now out of danger but was still suffering from severe mental stress. Ambuj also returned home. Poonam was yet to stay in the hospital.

□

Four

Yes, the unfortunate girl was 'Poonam' and was roughly around 18-20 years of age. She was neither fair nor dark but just the right complexion, she had sharp features with the sharp-pointed nose, was agile, doe-eyed that appeared as if they would speak.

The ravage of the poison had caused her flower-like delicate face to shrivel. However, her facial innocence was intact.

Destiny had taken away her parents from her when she was just a five-year-old kid. The auto-rickshaw, in which her parents were going, had collided with a truck that had gone out of control. The passengers, including the auto-rickshaw driver lost their lives, while Poonam was thrown out of the auto. The auto-rickshaw had turned into a scrap, and its ravages narrated the horrific impact of the accident. The unhurt body of Poonam surprised every bystander at the accident site.

Poonam was born into a joint family, where her father and uncle both jointly managed the inherited shops. Her old grandmother lived with them who would pray to the God every day to bring her to perish from the world, as she felt like a useless person ever since her husband had passed away.

The old woman aspired for the marriage of her younger son who had already reached the age of thirty but had remained a bachelor till then.

Somehow, her enthusiasm to get Naren, the younger son, married suddenly evaporated when she thought of the delicate little girl and her welfare.

"Oh God, bless me with a few more years of life till this little girl gets matured and then take my life." Again, such thoughts overpowered her and she started praying to the God.

The human mind is bizarre and sometimes the thought of controlling everything including life or death as per its command.

Since the consideration of the welfare of the orphaned girl was paramount in grandmother's mind, she just forgot about the urgency of the marriage of her grown up son.

"How will little Poonam be treated by the prospective wife of Naren?" was something that was disturbing the piece of mind of the old woman.

The excessive love showered on the orphaned girl by both grandmother and uncle somehow had made her a tad stubborn, which would trouble the grandma.

With falling business income, the demands and expectations of Poonam were rising day by day.

She would go to her school wearing clean-ironed dress, brightly polished shoes and a necktie and grandma would wish to take all misfortune to befall on her instead of Poonam.

Poonam's parents had wished her to be sent to the best school of the city to make her a doctor. The grandmother and the uncle made all-out efforts to twirl that dream of Poonam's parents into reality.

The grandma was old and suffered from gout problem and her gradually reducing eyesight. But she had to make sure of most of the chores concerning the girl, her granddaughter apart from cooking for all three of them. For the ailing grandma, the half-cooked lentils and vegetables devoid of any taste was mot a mystery anymore. She would sometimes leave 'chapatis' half baked. Ungrateful Poonam would often spit out the half-chewed food from her mouth and say, "I will not eat it." The grandmother and her uncle both would often sulk at her customary habit. The grandma would curse herself. "Hey, set my handicapped pair of hands on fire, as I am unable to satisfy the appetite of this small girl." To please the little one, her uncle would go and fetch milk and *jalebis* for her, which she would simply relish, while sitting on her grandma's lap. The grandma would cajole her further by saying "You, my little princess, eat what you wish to eat." The girl would ask "What this princess is all about?" The grandma would then narrate to her about the princess, the most cherished offspring to a 'Raja-Rani,' who lived in a grand palace, wore gold, diamond-laden clothes, and ate *milk-jalebi.* A good number of servants would surround the princess, run errand for her and obey all her dictates promptly. Poonam would ask then, "Am I that same princess grandma?" "Yes, you are that same princess," grandma would reply. "Then where is my palace?" The grandma would assure her of the palace saying one day, a prince would come from somewhere and take her to that palace. The image of that prince remained permanently etched in the little heart of the small girl. "How will you grow up and become strong by taking only milk and *jalebis*? Her uncle asked Poonam one day. He told her that she needed to eat good food to grow young. "Hey, how can I cook good food for you when even my hands tremble?" asked the grandma. Naren's marriage could only solve the problem for them. The only inhibition that prompted Naren to show his reluctance was how the prospective bride, Poonam's new aunt might treat little Poonam once she would join the family fold. The grandma said that she would keep a watch over her and ensure that no injustice was done to the orphan girl.

After a lot of deliberations and soul search, Naren agreed for the marriage with a beautiful and suave girl, Savitri, from a poor but respectable family.

As Savitri disembarked, she seized the all-inclusive responsibilities of the household including taking care of the little Poonam. She would efficiently sort out all the household chores in no time and would extend her support to the family business. The maternal instincts in Savitri surfaced to the core to cuddle little Poonam in her arms and take care of all her needs, providing motherly scaffold to the little girl and an intense feeling of satisfaction to the grandma. She thanked God for his blessings in providing her a daughter-in-law like Savitri, who hailed from a humble background.

'Had she belonged to a prosperous family, she would have thrown many tantrums, and would have been flaunting off the dowry brought by her. She is good-hearted and calm with a non-aggressive disposition like that of a cow. There had been no point of worry. If God pinches me now from this world, I will pass away peacefully.' The old woman was happy. She would pray to the God that she should leave this mortal world while her hands and feet were still moving. However, she could not grasp what was in store for little Poonam. Was he planting a bed of flowers for Poonam in the future, after he had brutally snatched everything from her? What was to happen now?

Unaware of this, entire grandmother was busy weaving her own dreams, the dreams about an illustrious future for Poonam.

The grandmother, who had lived blissfully mollified for almost one and a half years after Naren and Savitri's marriage, one day departed from the world for her heavenly abode. Savitri was the expecting mother in the family at that time. Human desires are not never-ending, nor do they grow old. The old woman wished to live a little longer to enjoy the company of her expected grandchild. However, the string of life is under no circumstances in the human being's hands but only in the hands of the Almighty.

After a few months, Savitri gave birth to a son and the house once again was filled with delight. Poonam was initially thrilled to applaud the arrival of the newborn but in next to no time she was spiteful of the little toddler felt in her bones the swing in her uncle and aunt's full attention from her. Little Poonam had been familiar with her aunt to be her mom, so even the slightest doling out of Savitri's affection, made her suffer with the excruciating pain.

Whenever Savitri would take the child on to her lap, Poonam would also take a pew on her lap.

"Look, how small is he? He is much younger than you are. Come on...sit on the bed."

"No, mother, I am still a fledgling. I have to sit on your lap."

Savitri encountered similar incidences of the Poonam's doggedness that slowly but surely incited Savitri with rage and ire; while it augmented, Poonam's even more.

The seed of discontentment soon deteriorated the sacrosanct bond between the mother and the daughter and Poonam, who was previously the apple of everyone's eye, had gradually become the sore of Savitri's eyes. She dredged upon the memories of that calendar day, the day when she had crossed the threshold of the family to take its reins just after her marriage. She had not even once comprehended that she was the daughter-in- law; precisely from bringing into existence her status as a cossetting mother to Poonam and lavishing care on her. With the advent of her own son, contraptions changed and Savitri organically developed indifference to the emotional nuts and bolts of little Poonam and developed a sneaking suspicion that she had grown jealous of Savitri's son.

When the second child comes into being after the first child, many families bump into this tight spot. Sibling rivalry is common among brothers and sisters and nothing special. The first child usually cannot tolerate the splitting up of that love, of which he is usually the sole owner, to be doled out with the other sibling, and all wise parents have to find the underlying cause of the issue to stumble on way outs.

Nevertheless, neither Savitri presented any sagacity nor Naren had any time on his hands to foresee any problem smothering their bonding from within. They felt assured that the warmth, with which they had been living earlier, persistently stuck around their home.

"Poonam is becoming defiant nowadays," Savitri opened her heart out to Naren when he arrived ahead of his accustomed schedule one day.

"How, what has she done?"

"She has become very stubborn."

"What's wrong with this? She is a child without her parents, my mother has raised her with a lot of love, she has to be a little stubborn," Naren did not anticipate the conundrum in precise earnest terms.

Furious Savitri preferred to say nothing, and the ensuing day something transpired that exacerbated the situation and tallied up fuel in the fire.

Poonam returned home from school with her face drenched with tears. Naren had come home for lunch.

"What happened to my daughter?"

"Mam has said...your dress is too dirty...shoes are too dirty and... your nails are not cut, and... if I visit the school in the same manner in future, she said...she will remove me from the school...she has also written a note in my diary."

Sobbing Poonam handed over the school diary to Naren.

"Savitri, can't you even dress up the girl properly? What has happened to you? See, what has the class teacher sent in writing?" Naren probed.

Exasperated Savitri at Naren's grievance bellowed in annoyance, vented her powerlessness after the arrival of the young member into the family on how could she confer her attention on Poonam.

"What work keeps you busy that you can't pay attention to Poonam's school clothes? Don't you know how my mother and I have looked after her; learn something from us who have never allowed any complaint from the school."

Savitri felt inclined to say something. Naren used to spin out his support to his mother in getting Poonam ready for the school, why does he withdraw the support to his wife, but Savitri refrained from saying anything, instead felt asphyxiated.

"Take care about it from now on, and Poonam, if you have any problem, let me know. I am there, right." While warning Savitri of the consequences, Naren afforded comforting assurance to Poonam.

Naren could not grasp the consequences of the blunder he made by voicing his reactions in presence of Poonam. While this act made Savitri feel her slipping under her feet, Poonam was encouraged.

The state of affairs continued to deteriorate. The geniality of Savitri's affable love that had kept Poonam nuzzled in the initial days soon lost its balminess became redundant. It is not that Savitri wished to end it with all her heart but Poonam's stubborn nature and Naren's intolerance worked together to crush her spirit.

More and more complaints started pouring from school whether regarding Poonam's homework, dirty clothes, unpolished shoes, etc. or her aggressive nature. Many parents came forward to protest, register their complaint against her hostility and abusiveness towards other children in the school.

Savitri, who initially listened seriously to Naren's admonishment, slowly but surely became acclimatize to it.

"Listen; there is some complaint or the other every day regarding Poonam's studies. Sometimes she doesn't do the Homework, on other occasions, she doesn't even do her classwork; she doesn't do her studies properly." Savitri was somehow crazed with a point of view that the operating expense of sending Poonam to a private school was excessively exhorbitant. Savitri waited for Naren's agreeable frame of mind before conjuring up a proposal of budging Poonam to a government school.

"Why send her to a government school? Why don't you teach her at home?" Naren asked Savitri.

Savitri gave a cunning smile and said, "Had I known English, I would have spoken gibberish English, and where do I have the time to teach?"

"So keep tuitions for her. My brother and sister-in-law had a desire that their daughter should study in the right school and becomes a doctor."

"Tuitions? He is now talking about the new expenditure, while the house's expenses are hardly met! Now, this princess will get tuitions."

Savitri thought in her mind, but now something has to be done for the newfangled conundrum.

"Does it not happen that children educated in government schools become doctors? Don't you know the son of the aunt of my sister-in-law? He has studied in the village government school until ninth and now understand, what a famous doctor he is today! I cannot even afford for her education at all," Savitri kept on saying so many things.

Naren just sighed, nodded and turned to sleep.

Savitri was pleased to think that the arrow had hit the target.

After constant nudging, fed-up Nareen pulled Poonam out of public school and enrolled her in a government school.

By this abrupt decision of the uncle, Poonam felt as if she had fallen from the sky. There was no comparison between the two schools. There was that school, where small kids sat on tiny tailor-made pieces of furniture and wore skirts, tie, and shiny shoes, and then there was this school, where the little kids were made to broom the school and were made to sit on the floor and would get torn mats to sit upon. Poonam always felt like revolting.

"I will not go to this school." It was announced on the very first day.

"So don't go, sit at home and share my load of household work." Hearing her aunt's response, Poonam shivered. What if her aunt really did that she had said?

She confided her feelings in her uncle but he also coaxed her to listen to her aunt. Poonam understood, now she has to go to this school. She simply could not sit at home. Poonam started going to the government school but haven't lost heart. When she used to see her friends going to the same school, it would smite her. She would feel a thorn deeply penetrated into some corner of her tiny heart, which would give her deep pain inside.

If the pain intensified, she would feel like asking her aunt, "Why did she kill her aspirations? Why has she made a servant of this princess, as she used to be when her grandmother was alive?"

Now, even her uncle was not in her favor, whom would she ask? Meanwhile, her aunt gave birth to a daughter. She had two small children to handle and the household work to top it all. She would get upset and in such a situation, she would seek out a formidable support system in Poonam.

Poonam would take care of a child whenever they would fall ill. She had to abstain herself from setting off to her school.

In irritation, Poonam would make children whimper.

"Why are they crying? What have you done?" her aunt would shriek in annoyance.

"I do not know? I did nothing." Poonam's expression would grow warped.

"You have grown up so much still can't even handle small children; you eat a whole heap but work a little," Savitri would lament with an expression of grief.

"If I don't know how to handle small children, why don't you take care of your children?" Poonam would say in reply. Poonam's rude repartee would often infuriate Savitri more, and then a situation came when Poonam was beaten and packed down by her aunt.

For the first time, when Savitri stroked Poonam with the whole palm, she felt terrible. She had raised up Poonam affectionately with love after her marriage, but now why was there so much acrimony cropped-up in their relationships?

"Kill me, cut me into pieces, but what you say, I will not do that. I will take revenge on you one day. Just observe this." When she saw Poonam's face aggressively inflamed with anger and smeared with tears, her anger would automatically melt away.

"Let this girl die," Savitri started using a harsh language for Poonam.

It was just the first time when she felt hesitant, and then it turned out to be a day-to-day affair.

Poonam would get involved in some kind of provocation to rage Savitri's anger, which she would thaw by stroking Poonam, and even then, Poonam would not hold back her tongue and resisted from spitting out the venom.

In the beginning, Poonam would complain to Naren regarding Savitri's concern. Later she felt that the complaints made by her were overshadowed by Savitri's objections. She had stopped taking uncle into confidence. Therefore, either he did not know the drama going on in his house, or if it occurred, he would take Savitri's favor. The same perception slowly became prominently etched in his mind that Poonam was the defiant.

Amid all these unpleasantness, Poonam passed her eighth examination. There was no time to study at home, but she would assimilate whatever was taught in the school due to the sharp intellect.

"Enough studying now. We don't have the strength to send you to the school further." Savitri raised her hands.

"But aunt!" Neither Savitri nor Poonam paid attention to when did Poonam's address to Savitri as 'mother' was changed to cold address as 'aunt'.

"But nothing, our own expenses are met with great difficulty, now help us in household work."

"Aunt, this is a government school. Girls do not have to pay fees there." Poonam's face appeared insipid. What is going to be her future!

"Hey! The saying has been as if the cost of studies is only school fee. Books, clothes, and other expenses are also required and we do not have that now," Savitri said.

"Auntie, I have to study anyway."

She is speaking as if her father had left the property and gone away and left this sneaky girl for us.

"Don't bring me, father in the middle."

Finally, this debate ended with a slap on Poonam's cheek. Poonam already knew that this would happen, she had become accustomed to it but she did not even imagine what happened that evening.

"I can't live in this house with this girl anymore." Savitri declared.

Naren understood that there was a fight between the two. He had heard many times from Savitri that Poonam was getting stubborn but since he wished to avoid any discord in the house, he would always remain silent. At the same time, however, the challenges related to business had never stopped chasing him.

"I have no one in this house. I will go to my maternal house with both the children and then uncle and niece will live here peacefully." Whenever there was an argument between Poonam and Savitri, these words would automatically come out from Savitri's mouth.

Naren got irritated when Savitri repeated the same line one more time.

"Now, what has happened today?" asked Naren.

"Hey, you ask me what hasn't happened. Savitri retorted in a sharp tone. You just get an eligible boy and get her married. When she leaves this house, only then will she get peace of mind. Savitri said in an almost crying manner.

"Marry her! She is just fifteen years only," Naren was surprised. Poonam and Savitri did not mix up well, and now Savitri was dominating Poonam.

"Oh yes, by your reckoning, she is just a smell kid! I say get her married soon otherwise she is going to defame all of us," Savitri get furious.

Savitri revealed another side of Poonam, she said we belonged to a lower-middle-class family, where grooming and beautifying growing-up girls is considered wrong.

Savitri, however, had told all lies. It was not like that. Poonam was fond of fashionable dresses and liked to dress well. As she progressed in age, urge to dress well continued to develop. She did not have many clothes, but whatever clothes she had, she kept them well, and after washing them, she used to keep them spotlessly clean, and she would fold them nicely. If her aunt did not iron her clothes, she would fold the clothes under the pillow. She would often use her aunt's make-up material secretly.

It was not straightforward to grasp to see the point of what had been taking place in Poonam's mind. Uncle's income was not enough. Although, he owned a small shop, he could barely meet the household expenses. His both children were of school-going age and their educational expenses were phenomenal. When Poonam would see her uncle's children go to school in a school uniform, wearing well-polished school shoes, she would get very upset. Why was she removed from her earlier school? She would ponder over this repeatedly. When she looked at the children from the affluent families, aspirations within her would start galloping with the fleeting speed. She craved she had been born in a big house and had been a princess, and would have studied until she desired and would have acquired a higher status through her education, but this could never be brought to fruition for her. She would blurt out her frustrating emotions from within embroiled in a verbal duel with her aunt. She had stomached corporeal punishment several times for pocketing her aunt's make-up, but even then, her innermost desires had not ceased to exist.

The aunt was in the kitchen at night. Seeing her uncle alone, she sat near him.

"Uncle, I wish to study further; arrange that, I must go to a school." While talking to her uncle, tears rolled out from her eyes.

Uncle looked at her carefully for the first time and wished to grasp what his wife had alleged. Well-worn clothes, neatly adorned hair, and long streaks of tears flowing from the eyes to the cheeks.

"Poonam has really started indulging in fashion. Savitri had been right in saying that," Naren thought to himself but the thereafter when he got the drift of her tears, he commiserated with his orphaned niece. Anyways, she merely wanted to bone up to complete her education starved of any arbitrary exigency.

"I'll talk to your aunt." Uncle left, stroking his head with a hand.

Poonam understood that not anything substantial would crop up. She was aware of her aunt's response and comprehensively from top to bottom had discerned her uncle's authority and the courage!

Her uncle entered the kitchen and tossed his fleeting look on Savitri. She looked quite stern. Naren somehow mustered audacity to have a tête-à-tête about furtherance of Poonam's education. "Poonam wants to study further; she must have had a word with you too?" Naren had marshaled an adequate amount of courage to verbalize this. "Yes, but I refused. The financial condition of our family is not favorable. Moreover, she barely manages to make the grades in her exams. What would she do by going to school, she can privately engage in her further studies," Savitri retorted.

"Poonam, your aunt, is right; you can privately pull off

your further studies." While saying this, Naren had erased his brother and sister-in-law's nourished desire to make their daughter a doctor from his mind. It could not be conceivably accomplished without attending the school.

Moreover, what happened after that was unexpected; Naren never thought that Poonam could go to such an extent. "Wife's slave." The words spurted out from Poonam's mouth as an upshot of extreme frustration and steaming ire that she had retained within.

In reaction to Poonam's spiteful comment, Naren spanked her in frenzy.

That night, except the children of the house, none could eat anything. Naren had started speculating seriously, like Savitri, the notion that Poonam was turning out to be audaciously insolent with every passing day.

□

Five

Naren and his family lived in their ancestral house of three rooms, a small kitchen, and a courtyard. One breathing space that was legitimately identified as a verifiable drawing- room embodied five to six chairs, a table, and a box-bed. Another room belonged to Savitri and her husband, and the third room that had been grandmother and Poonam's room, was agreed to as Poonam and children's room. If any guest would visit them, then that room would be jerked from Poonam, or it can be implied that Poonam would vacate that room to move out to the storeroom, which stockpiled many of the house's pieces of stuff.

Apart from this ancestral house, there was a small shop, run by Poonam's great-grandfather, then her grandfather, and later was owned by Poonam's father and subsequently by her uncle. Luckily, Poonam's great-grandfather and grandfather were the only sons of their parents, so the matters of dividing the immovable property like shop and house never emerged.

Savitri had many vicious plans under her sleeves; one of them was an intention to lease out the room on rent, which she had expressed to Naren one day, which he could not understand.

When Naren probed, "Where are the rooms to rent?" Savitri unconsciously retorted, "Poonam's room! The door of that room moreover opens on the outside."

"But our luggage? Moreover, where will Poonam go?" Naren asked.

"Where will she go? She has been staying with us for so long; she will continue to remain here. Besides, where is the lack of space here? We will keep some stuff in the room. As far as Poonam's sleep is concerned, she will sleep on the small wooden bed outside."

"But who will take a room?"

"Hey, why don't you? Find a student to live in it, he does not have to cook and will not have much stuff. We will be able to keep our belongings there as well," Savitri suggested the trick.

"But...?" Naren still had doubts.

Now leave this reasoning. We will start finding tenants from tomorrow onwards. If we can get some more money, then household needs would be effortlessly accomplished. Anyway, we have to get her married soon also," Savitri wanted to end the talk skillfully to calm down Naren.

Two months later, a tenant had arrived for that room. He had taken admission in a pharmacy college in the city last year. He had stayed in the hostel for one year, but liked neither the atmosphere there nor the food. When a friend told him about this house, he reached here and rented that room, which was to his liking.

His name was Raghvendra. He was the only scion of a landlord's family of the Terai region. He was a second-year student in pharmacy. After enjoying the facilities available to his family, how could he have enjoyed living in the small college hostel, hence decided on the rented accommodation? He wished to make a bright future in pharmacy for himself by performing excellently to fetch the degree and study further. He needed to get good numbers in the degree course. The house's financial condition was so healthy that he was in no hurry time pressure to look for a job.

Initially, Poonam had loads of unrest due to the tenant's arrival, but what could she do? She gradually tried to adapt to the changed circumstances. After misbehaving with her uncle, she exhausted his love and compassion for her.

Raghvendra continued to dine at a hotel, but later due to Savitri's insistence, he started eating there—he had become a paying guest. Savitri also started earning extra income.

Poonam was now seventeen years old, and her aunt was actively ferretting around for a matrimonial alliance for her. In all this humdrum of activities, the genuine issue of her education somehow died down. However, she knew that expenses would also be high to accomplish a well-thought-of marriage in a well-thought-of family. Somehow, Savitri wanted to get rid of Poonam, who had been more of a problem for her, even though she was required to cough up extravagant expenditures.

"Aunt, I don't want to get married yet." One day she mustered courage to treat with contempt the idea of marriage, after hearing uncle and aunt talk about it.

"So what will you do?" her aunt rubbernecked at her with devouring stares.

"Do you want to become a ruler by accomplishing your education?" Aunt asked all over again.

"I don't want to be a queen, but I definitely want to stand on my own feet." Poonam wanted to say this but could not say it.

Poonam, who was her grandma's princess, was nowhere to be found, and what had been stayed instead was an infuriating spoilt girl whom the aunt wished to get herself liberated from her in some way.

This was really the case. However, the dreams were not completely broken yet. Although, becoming a doctor was no longer possible, the prince of her dreams would still charm her sometimes and move in his palace with her.

Savitri would infrequently send Poonam in the evening to offer Raghvendra his meals. However, whenever she went to his room to give him food, she would always find him deeply immersed in his books. Seeing he engrossed in his studies, her desire to accomplish her education would coagulate in her. It had gradually become her destiny to remain engaged in household chores, but her aspirations had not shattered yet.

"What books do you read?" One day Poonam dared to ask Raghvendra. Raghvendra replied, "Pharmacy" while still engrossed in his books, Poonam could not conjecture anything. Raghvendra's indifference hurt her. Her expectations were unconvincingly far-fetched. "What difference would it make if he somewhat speaks to her," she would frequently speculate.

Continuously for some days, she brought him food but he remained unresponsive. However, Raghvendra noticed her insolent behavior but remained undesirous to discern the purpose, nor did it matter to him. Poonam possessed an approach that did not concede her to bow down.

Now, Raghvendra initiated the talk.

"In which class do you study?" Raghvendra had nothing else to talk about, hence, asked the same question to start the conversation.

"I don't go to school." "What does that mean?"

"I have to discontinue my studies."

"Till which class has you studied?"

"Eighth. It has been many years since I passed my eighth."

"Why, why haven't you studied further?"

"Aunt did not grant me permission. But I love to study."

"Then why don't you clear your tenth class from the open board?"

"What is that?"

Suddenly she heard her aunt called out her name 'Poonam' in a shrill voice that she immediately ran away from there.

For the first time, hesitant Poonam and Raghvendra had a little conversation regarding her education that defrosted the initial glitch and paved a concrete path for further discussion.

Poonam was now waiting for the next opportunity when she could have taken meals for him. That whole day she deemed as if the entire day had been too long and she repeatedly checked on the clock that ticked slowly, or if it did, it hardly seemed to tick. She also felt the speed of the needle had slowed down today. As if, the sun had refused to set down today.

The evening had descended into night, but Poonam was unreasonably fidgety, for she did not know why the aunt was taking so long to cook that day. Poonam's edginess unrelentingly continued to escalate over time. After a long time, when her aunt entered the kitchen, Poonam also walked along with her.

Aunt gave vegetables to Poonam to cut, and she left the kitchen. When she returned, Poonam had already cut vegetables and kneaded the flour.

"Today, you are working very quickly. What's the matter with you? How has it affected the lazy person like you today?" Her aunt quipped in a satiric tone.

Had it been some other day, Poonam would have replied with a stinging repartee, but today she smiled instead and kept quiet.

So that her aunt does not have any doubt about her demeanor, Poonam herself refused to serve food for Raghvendra.

"Why won't you go and give food to him. You! Ominous woman! You don't do any work until you are not told." When her aunt yelled at her, Poonam quickly lifted the plate and walked towards Raghvendra's room as if she waited for this opportunity. "What is this open board, and how can I appear for my tenth exam?" The moment she kept the plate of food on the table, she aimed her question at Raghvendra, a question that had mentally consumed her since the previous night.

"You don't have to go to school on this. You can appear for your exams by studying at home."

"But where can one get its form from, and when are they filled?" Poonam inquired hurriedly.

"Nowadays, forms are being filled." Raghvendra replied. In the small but informative meeting with Raghvendra, Poonam had been enlightened about continuing with further studies without going to school. When she realized this, it provided luminous wings to her imagination. She would study, do a job, her money would come into her hands, strengthen her and she will become financially independent. While visualizing this dream, Poonam eagerly awaited the next day for Raghvendra, who would have brought examination form and books for her, for she had entrusted this work to him.

She could hardly wait for the next day, so when Raghvendra started going to college on the second day, it appeared her imagination had kicked off in full swing. She bounced out of the room on some pretext and did not forget to hark back at Raghvendra to bring the forms and books.

Reluctantly, Raghvendra obeyed her and brought her

form and books. Poonam's mind was stirred-up with ecstasy. Before tucking herself in bed at night, Poonam had read the document from one edge to the other. She overturned the books several times and eventually fell asleep, weaving sweet dreams about her future.

For a few days, she kept both the form and the books hidden from view. After all, permission to test was to be obtained from both her uncle and aunt. For this, she was looking for an appropriate time. The uncle would agree, but it was difficult to convince the aunt. However, this time she too was not ready to give up.

Sooner her aunt finished her food and went to her room, Poonam followed her and placed her point before her.

Savitri looked at her carefully. No, this was not Poonam, who never even spoke softly was speaking in a sugarcoated voice.

"Aunt, I will do all the household works. You won't have any problem." She folded her hands before Savitri. She knew that there was no choice.

When she came face-to-face with both her uncle and aunt, Poonam got on to her feet to convince her persuasively with folded hands. When her aunt surreptitiously eyeballed her to scrutinize her face, Poonam was shivering and had mentally evoked the divine blessings of God.

Unpredictably, Savitri appeared to have been personified in a wistful state of affairs. She was clueless regarding her situation that day. She felt like unleashing Poonam of her superciliousness, to forgive her from all her erstwhile moments of conceited arrogance and let her do whatever she wished to do.

After all, Poonam's stratagem had been efficaciously accomplished. The uncle had been silent all this while, but the aunt of her own accord bequeathed her consent. Poonam's happiness knew no bounds and she jumped in elation. At the spur of the moment, she fell on her aunt's feet in due reverence to grab her benedictions, and this time, she was not following her plan, but whole-heartedly, with genuine happiness.

Even Savitri could not discern what she liked in that situation. However, the glowing tears in Poonam's eyes gave the impression of being like precious pearly droplets to her. Although, she had wished to put her hand of benevolence on orphaned Poonam's head, she, somehow, did not do that. Poonam was happy, thrilled. The next day, after completing the form, she handed it over to Raghvendra for submission. Poonam had started her studies in full swing, and Raghvendra rallied around to assist her with her homework. It had been many years since she had left her studies, so her reading habits had been lost. Raghvendra again came forward to support her, explaining to her how to study. Taking a cue from her own example and mode of study, he told her how to check for hours together.

Poonam was indebted to Raghvendra. This was, after a long time, someone had spoken to her since her grandmother had left. Poonam could also be held accountable for shaking off the love of the rest of the family members. Poonam, who had always yearned for the adorations of her loved ones, slowly started pulling towards Raghvendra, who was unaware of Poonam's feelings for him, but what had happened to Savitri.

Savitri, keeping surveillance on Poonam's every movement, would scrutinize her clothes, makeup, tricks, and tests everything around her, here seemed to have missed ascertaining any slight difference in her gestures. Why did Poonam, who always talked to her irritatingly, have to turn out to be nimbler like a flower? Why would she burst into laughter at the slightest inkling? Her aunt would assign whatever work to her; she would blithely accomplish that task without any demurral. Savitri did not see this change, or perhaps she continued to understand that probably her acquiescence to Poonam's continuation of her education has done the trick.

Savitri would sulk when Poonam would study until late at night, for she had no idea how much electricity would be incurred. However, she confided her apprehensions to Naren regarding the electricity expenses' escalation, but he postponed it.

"Poonam, why don't you study during the day?" When she could not resist, she told her one day.

"Aunt, there is a lot of noise during the day, you can read peacefully at night, it also makes sense. In the day, it diverts attention."

Poonam knew and understood why her aunt was formulating a suggestion like that, but she silently retained the sense of her own good.

"Just, somehow, after completing my further studies and financially becoming independent, then I will tell the aunt." She thought to herself and preferred to remain quiet. Poonam passed her tenth with a good percentage even without entering school formally. Her heart pulsated with excitement. She wished to give this news first to Raghvendra, but he had been off to his hometown for the holidays. Poonam started counting the days of his return. Her uncle was also exultant with her success, except for Savitri, who remained nonchalant with her success. Poonam's enthusiasm was at its peak. She could now see in her mind's eye the actualisation of her dreams. She had two objectives to be fulfilled—the accomplishment of her education and her prince Raghvendra.

When Raghvendra returned after spending the holidays, hundreds of lotuses blossomed on Poonam's face. She reached his room immediately with the marks-sheet.

"I have passed, see my marks-sheet." While she confided her exhilaration with Raghvendra, hundreds of fireflies could be seen shining in Poonam's eyes. The joy of sharing her success with her most loved person was evident on her face.

"Very good!" After seeing her marks-sheet, Raghvendra patted her head lightly in appreciation. He felt good and proud of Poonam's accomplishment as well as his assistance to accomplish her dream. Although, in the beginning, when Poonam would repeatedly enter his room every now and then to seek his help or explain the solution to her problems, it would irritate him, for he would do his studies. He was on cloud nine after realizing Poonam's exuberance of success.

Moreover, Poonam was keen on Raghvendra's glee. The picture of Raghvendra, which had been buried in one corner of her consciousness, turned out to be evidently distinct.

"What do I do next?" Raghvendra was his mentor and his friend.

"Twelfth, you can do it like you finished your tenth." "And then?" Poonam's aspirations now had wings. After that, B.A. and what?

"And then will I get a job after doing B.A." "Probably not."

"Then, what is the use of education?"

"If you want to study, it is better to do some course rather than doing twelfth or B.A., to do a job."

"Which course can I do?" Poonam asked curiously. "Learn typing or take a nursing course. This will get you to work."

"Why, nurse? Why not a doctor? Poonam's aspiration started scampering rapidly.

"Idiot! To become a doctor, you need to mandatorily pass your twelfth with science stream, and one has to go to school daily." Raghvendra laughed at her understanding. The light on Poonam's face was soon extinguished.

Poonam had not dreamt of a job as a typist or a nurse. She was disappointed, for her dreams were much higher than becoming a typist or a nurse, almost touching the sky.

The human mind is bizarre. When the scope of obtainability is diminished, the mind wishes to acquire the inconsequential, but as soon as the fresh avenues of feats open up, it battles to get much more. Poonam underwent the same set of state of affairs. For her, the continuation of her education after completing eighth had been in itself a mammoth challenge and getting permission from Savitri a humongous task. Surprisingly, then, Poonam's simplest wish had been to just go to school and continue her primary education. On the other hand, the moment she finished her tenth standard through the open board, her mind started slithering through the glades of aspirations faster than the speed of her mind.

Nevertheless, even after taking a nursing and typing course, she had to venture out of her home into the world. Would Savitri give her permission to pursue those courses? Besides, how would she incur the expenses?

"Aunt won't let me do anything." Poonam sounded disillusioned, "First, she will not let me go out from home, and then if she would be ready in some way, then the cost of these courses will be very high."

"Try to explain once. Who knows, your aunt might agree?" While Raghvendra said to Poonam, she nodded in affirmation.

"Will you bring me the nursing form by then?" She requested Raghvendra.

"Yes, I will bring it, but first, you talk to your uncle and aunt." Raghvendra replied, vexed by Poonam's repeated pleadings, buoying up his equipoise and mood.

Raghvendra left the hostel and decided to stay in a separate accommodation for the sake of his studies. He had assumed that he would be able to study without any disturbance in a different room, but Poonam would sometimes bother him badly. He would also get angry, but when he would see orphan Poonam, he would feel pity for her and maintained the norm of facilitating her precisely because of the same kindness. He could not even guess even in his dreams what had been transpiring in Poonam's mind regarding him.

One day after getting a chance, Poonam laid bare her feelings in front of Savitri.

"Aunt, I want to take up a nursing course."

Savitri looked carefully at Poonam. What has happened to her? She had given Poonam permission to appear for her class tenth examinations, she had started taking undue advantage of her kindness.

"What is this new rote that you have caught? Your uncle is looking for a suitable match for you. Enough of studying till the tenth," her aunt stared at her.

"But I don't want to get married right now." Poonam shivered as soon as she heard the name of marriage. She did not know whom they would get her married to. Raghvendra's face swirled in his eyes, and then she still wished to be financially independent.

"Then what will you do?" Savitri's voice became bitter.

"I will study further. I wish to stand on my feet and will then think of getting married." Savitri also felt the tenacity in Poonam's voice.

"Will study! Do a job! You will earn money, and what

will be the cost of doing the course? Then we have to marry you too. Your parents have left you; we will have to fulfill our duty. This way, we will not let you remain unmarried. Go and wash the dishes. You think yourself to be a big scholar." The aunt had pronounced her decision. It was not very easy to change. Poonam was aware of the outcome, and in a fit of anger, she felt like breaking all the utensils in the house but refrained from doing it. However, gripped in the same mood and anger, the sound of washing dishes became more noticeable.

"Hey, will you break the utensils?" When she heard her aunt's shouting, Poonam caught the inkling. Why is she venting her anger on these lifeless utensils? It would have been better had she been thinking of something else. However, she decided to stop the marriage first.

On the same evening, when she entered Raghvendra's room with his dinner, tears came rolling out of her eyes with angry expressions on her face.

"They won't let me study." "Why, what did your aunt say?"

"Where will the expenses come from?" Poonam's voice appeared to emanate as if from the deep recesses as deep as the well.

Although Poonam kept running to his room repeatedly and disturbing Raghvendra in his studies, after she left the room, he kept thinking about her situation for a while. Sometimes this feeling of helping her seemed to have distracted him from his purpose. However, Poonam's tears had moved him once again. When she wants to study, why do her uncle and aunt object to this? Their own children were studying in a public school. How could he help her? He kept pondering.

"Poonam, is this your uncle's house?" He asked, just like that.

"I do not know. It is ancestral house."

"And what about the shop?"

"I don't even know that, but what I know is that it was first run by my grandfather, then by my father and now uncle." Poonam could not fathom Raghvendra's intentions.

"If this property is ancestral, then it belongs equally to your father and uncle. Your father is no more, now. Therefore, his share belongs to you. It's your right too. Speak to them; they would bear your expenses from your share of the property." Raghvendra suggested another way.

"But how will it happen? They have raised me, and they will pay for my wedding too." Poonam started trembling from within the moment she heard what Raghvendra had suggested.

"So, what happened? The marriage doesn't cost that much, and then you don't have to get married early, you have to study first. Marriage can wait."

These things had never entered her mind. In fact, it never occurred to her that even she was the stakeholder in their house and shop. When Raghavendra referred to her stake in the paternal property, it settled in some corner of her mind.

"Raghavendra is right." She has a share in this house and shop and look at the aunt. She treats her worse than a house cleaner.

The princess was not getting the palace, but the feeling of being the mistress of half of this small house filled her with pride.

Poonam could not sleep that whole night.

She kept recalling the words of Raghvendra repeatedly with an upheaval of thoughts in her mind. Poonam might have been exceedingly stubborn, even though she hated her aunt, but she was, after all, a human being and not so young that she could not discern between the good and the bad. By the way, Raghavendra has suggested the right way, but... However, will she be able to do it? Will she be able to speak about her share in front of her uncle and aunt? No! Will she dare to do this? After all, they have brought her up since her childhood, and they have further responsibilities to perform.

Nevertheless, her future's question also flashed through her mind, she wanted to study right, but her aunt wanted to destroy her future even before it was established. She had always been complaining about the lack of money. After all, why she should not fight for her rights?

Many such questions kept erupting in her mind, and she would beget answers from within.

So, what? In return for her share of the property, they had brought her up. Otherwise, who cares for anyone in this world? If they financially support her in doing a course, then what is the big deal? After all, that property is to be owned by them later.

Poonam finally decided claim her right fearlessly in a heart-to-heart discourse with her uncle and aunt,.

In the morning, after finishing her household chores, she went to her aunt.

"Aunty ...!" She mustered up the courage.

"Yes! I am listening! ..." Savitri looked at her with a furtive glance while thinking about what she was up to then. Poonam had some strange expressions on her face.

Poonam had risen obstinately in revolt against Savitri and her decision.

"Aunt, I know how the expenses for my education can be met."

"Tell me?" Savitri had roasted, by this time, on envisioning her expressions.

Looking at her confident expressions, her aunt discerned to herself trying to guess what treasure Poonam had explored. Nevertheless, Savitri could not grasp even in her wildest of dreams what Poonam had been demanding. Savitri had been brought up in a lower-middle-class family, and her sacraments prohibited her from demanding her share in her father's property. She had ritualistically considered the daughters to be someone alien to their father's house. Her parents' expenditures in the marriage have always been considered her share in the father's property.

"Aunt, can you please financially support my course in return for my share in the house and shop," Poonam reiterated hurriedly, for had she wasted crucial time thinking, she would have never said it.

These words spoken by Poonam felt like an explosion. What had Poonam said, and from where did she gather so much courage? Who told her that this could also happen? Savitri was sure that it couldn't have been originated in her mind. Who could be that person? Whom does she meet? She could not think of any name, even in her remotest imagination. Moreover, Poonam stays at home all day long. "Raghvendra! Probably him! Is she committing some kind of lapse by sending Poonam to him every day with the dinner? Yes, it was a mistake Savitri, who had always considered herself very smart, had been defeated at her own game.

Savitri was upset all day long. When she had entered into the family after getting married, Poonam was a small child, she had brought her up and provided her with primary education following their ability. They had planned to get Poonam married and looked forward to some suitable match for her. However, what was that which Poonam had said? Has she forgotten all relationships? Now she has become so big and sensible that she has started asking for a share in the shop. It had not happened until date that any girl had asked for a stake in her father's property.

"This girl has lost her mind again. Don't know which spirit has possessed her," her aunt thought to herself in exasperation.

Savitri's ire repeatedly reiterated on her face, at Poonam's ultimatum for her share in the paternal property but did not say anything. She deemed it respectable to have a dialogue with her husband over the controversial matter. In the evening, when Naren came from the shop, she was waiting with the latest presumption of Poonam to tell him. Poonam's complaint had been emerging many times

in the past, but this time the matter was serious.

Naren was shocked to hear what Poonam had to say. Whatever tussle had been going on between Savitri and Poonam, but he never rebuked her in a loud voice. He had always lived under his wife's pressure, and to save the house from strife, he preferred to keep quiet. However, today Poonam has crossed the limit. He was very angry with her.

"Call her. She had got so courageous that she had failed to respect the sanctity of their relationship." Savitri had seen Naren losing his temper at Poonam for the first time.

Poonam had emerged fearless, adventuresome, and there was no sign of dread and ignominy on her face. Naren was flabbergasted to see the new appearance of her. So far, he had forgotten Savitri's grievances as Poonam's childish prank. Savitri, on the other hand, relentlessly complained, sometimes complained about stealing money from the house and sometimes for her rude behavior of countering back. However, Naren did not try to dilate the matter between Savitri and Poonam and left it as their mutual matter. Now, it had gone severely beyond the limit.

From where had the little girl taken the idea that she also possessed a share in the house?

Poonam was now standing in front of Naren.

"Poonam, what is your aunt saying? What am I listening to?"

"Uncle, I have to take a nursing course. I want to study further and stand on my feet."

"So, you need your share of shop and house to do the course?" Naren asked the question.

"If you do not wish to give me my share, provide me with money to exchange for it. I will live my own life." There was a sense of ridicule in her voice.

"Your life! Is your life different from mine? Will we ever think anything bad for you? We were thinking of settling you down, but who has put these things in your mind." Naren got into thinking.

"No one, I have to study and think about myself. You don't have money, so I said this." Poonam answered point-blank.

Naren was left speechless, astounded, and indignant. He was confused what to do, what not to do, for his niece was also not wrong. Where had he denied that she too possessed a share in the property?

Nevertheless, this was not the way to demonstrate authority.

He missed his toddler Poonam, who was left without her parents. He remembered that Poonam, who could not sleep without a swing in his uncle's arms, remembered that Poonam wore clothes ironed by Naren with his own hands and would drop her at school. He thought whether Poonam had forgotten everything but Naren had not forgotten anything. Just a little dust had settled over the period over memory, but the memories were not very blurred. Naren's eyes filled with tears, and he turned his face to the other side, while Poonam also turned around on the other side, but her reason was completely different. She did not wish to become weak after seeing her teary-eyed uncle. Neither had she wanted to. She could currently see only her half share of this house just and nothing else.

Seeing the silence of Naren, Savitri had to take charge. "Listen, I understand this girl has gone out of hand.

Before she brings dishonor to our family, marry her. Moreover, hear me, girl! Don't step out of your room from today itself. You don't even have to take food for Raghvendra."

Naren was shocked to hear Raghvendra's name. He thought Raghvendra had induced her for wrongdoings like this. He was thinking evil of a benefactor. They had thought they would ask him to vacate the house.

A few days ago, Savitri received a marriage proposal for Poonam. The boy was a widower and had a daughter from his first marriage. He was still young and belonged to a prosperous family. He wanted simple marriage ceremonies in the house in the presence of a handful of people.

Even though greediness emanated in Savitri's mind, her husband would not consent to it, she knew this. Therefore, she never told him about the marriage proposal. However, that day, she blurted the news about the proposal in anger. "Now go to your house and do what you do. Tell your husband that you do not do household work. Do not raise children, but have study only."

Impatience and anger emerged on Poonam's face and tears rolled out from her eyes. In a state of rage, she had forgotten that if she would apologize to her uncle, he could still accept it. Poonam, who had lost the power to deliberate and cognize, and had forgotten the norms of consideration and respect, was also not ready to step down in humility, as this was against her pride.

At this time, Raghvendra appeared to be her downright well-wisher. Poonam irresistibly misconstrued his sympathy, kindness, and his affinity as love. She felt that even if she would revolt against her uncle and aunt, Raghavendra would still be with her.

Poonam did not take food that night. Although Savitri and Naren did not say anything humiliating, she went to bed crying. There was no iota of the snooze in her eyes. Now, what she could do or what she could not? Repeatedly this question nagged her. She would grab her right. What could be her next step? What would happen if her aunt would get her married before that? So, what would happen to her life? What would happen to the dream that she has seen? She could not find an answer to her questions.

"Raghvendra" Yes, Raghvendra could only help her get rid of this problem.

Shortly after the lights of uncle-aunt's room were dimmed, she got up and stood at the door of Raghvendra's room. She could see the light of his room from the crinkles of the door. She nonchalantly tapped at the door when Raghavendra was studying. The darkness of the night encompassed pin drop tranquility; the wearied neighborhood was in a profound repose when Raghavendra was astounded by a knock for a moment. He was bewildered, where in the stability of the darkness, the voice had emanated from. When he again listened to the agent, then only could he grasp. Poonam was standing in front of the door. He immediately looked at the ticking clock; it was one o'clock in the night.

Poonam's condition was also strange. Her eyes were brimmed with tears, desperation loomed large on her face, and after hours of persistent crying, her eyes had been swollen.

"What happened to her? Why has she come to him at this unearthly hour?" Before he could decipher anything, Poonam had already hugged him.

"Take me away from here, Raghav. Everybody is my enemy, here; nobody will allow me to do anything."

Raghavendra was taken by surprise. What was Poonam saying? Where should he take her and why?

"But why?" He said, separating Poonam from him.

"You have helped me a lot Raghav. Now help me a little more. Take me somewhere away from this house. I want to study, live my life the way you want it. These people will marry me to someone else."

"To someone else?" Raghvendra shocked. So does Poonam want to get married somewhere else?

"Yes, Raghav, to someone else. To a person who is already the father of a daughter. Now you tell me what do I do?"

"So, do you want to marry someone else?" asked Raghvendra.

This awkward question by Raghvendra to Poonam was as if she had fallen from the sky.

Why is Raghvendra asking that? Doesn't he know whom she should marry? Does he expect her to say everything herself? Thinking about her feelings, she felt embarrassed to identify her emotions and simultaneously decided to evade that embarrassment for the time being and confided everything clearly to Raghvendra.

"What are you saying, Raghav? I want to marry you."
"Married to me!" Raghvendra looked shocked as if he had touched a naked electric wire.

"What are you saying, Poonam. I never said that. I was just helping you. I was guiding you in the right direction. Right now, I cannot even think about it. I have to study a lot right now."

Poonam was silent. Suddenly, her tears stopped rolling down her cheeks. The temperature of both her cheeks had suddenly increased. Tears dried up. Poonam's condition at that point was such that he could not be reprimanded. It was respectable enough to put it in plain words and illuminate upon it. He grabbed her by her shoulders and seated her there on the wooden board.

"Poonam, you are a good girl. You wish to study which is a good thing. I just provided you with directions. It is your job to convince your family members. Whether you do it with love or rebellion, it is your choice. I have just advised you, when I saw your desire to study and nothing more. However, you want to live your life your own way depending on your share of the property, it doesn't seem appropriate. What is your age right now? How difficult is it for a single girl to stay out alone, do you know that? What support can I give you? My own future is not determined yet. You go to your room now; it is very late now."

Whatever Raghvendra had said, Poonam could partially grasp to a certain extent. At that instant, it seemed as if she was under the forceful grip of the devil incarnate, which had somewhat condensed her power to understand and think. In this state of mind, her vocal sound intensified into a loud deafening sound. The more Raghvendra instructed her to repress her voice and observe silence, the more she would speak in a more audible tone.

The thickness of stretched, nighttime tranquility was strewn all around, occasionally broken by the barking of the stray dogs. When most people had been sleeping, Poonam and Raghvendra were debating in that room of the house, which had ineludibly made Raghvendra paranoid about the whole situation. Disgruntled with hostel arrangements, he had taken a rented accommodation for studies to evade those set of circumstances, and now, here, it had become a mess. As Poonam had no control over herself, moreover, Raghvendra's rebuttal made her feel like her dream had been shattered. Poonam could talk about her rights in front of her uncle and aunt, only because Raghvendra had relentlessly supported her. The debate that had stemmed from desperation and the escalating voice had pierced the room's walls and fell on Savitri's ears. What happened after that was very bad. Savitri had also brought Naren with her. Audacious Poonam was not affected by any new development, but Raghavendra suffered like being incapacitated by unexpected fright. He kept representing his version with countless clarifications, but none of them paid attention to his recital of account.

Naren even spanked Raghvendra to the pulp.

□

Six

The next morning was the same for everyone, but it was very different in Naren's house. Raghvendra had emptied the room early in the morning itself since he hardly possessed much stuff anyway, just some clothes and books that he had bagged and could shift in an auto to another place. The neighbourhood people could scarcely get an inkling of the storm conspired in their house that night and what had shattered them.

Naren had left for the shop after giving instructions to lock Poonam in a room, whereas Poonam had not taken her breakfast nor opened the door for anyone.

Naren had not come home even for lunch, nor Savitri cared for Poonam due to a busy schedule. When Naren returned at night, he asked about Poonam.

"Where will she be! Lying in her room. Does she have any face to show?"

"Did she eat anything?" Naren's concern could be ascertained through the anxiety in his words.

"No. I do not like to see Poonam's face." Savitri's resentment towards Poonam had not calmed down yet.

"Never mind, I too possess a lot of wrath against her, but if she stops eating and drinking like this, then it will worsen the situation. Come on, you bring the food I will call her. We can converse too with her and try to fathom what has been going on in her mind."

Forgiveness is obligatory for the elders, and rage goes well with the little ones. Naren was following this path, but Savitri did not like it. What happened next was nothing short of a terrible nightmare. Naren knocked at the door, called out her name, but there was no response from inside. Savitri and Narendra both got scared when it was a little late.

"What are you waiting for? Break open the door." Panicked by Poonam's threat, Savitri had said to Naren.

The dilapidated door could not bear the little push by Naren. What they saw inside the room was beyond their imagination, Savitri screamed out in panic.

In one corner of the room, Poonam was lying fainted with her mouth foaming, and an empty pouch of rat poison was lying on the floor nearby.

Nervous, Naren tried his best to waggle Poonam, splashed her face with a splatter of water to bring Poonam back into consciousness, but all in vain. He ran outside.

"Where are you going?" Savitri stopped Naren.

"To bring an auto, we have to take her to the hospital; we do not know when she took this poison; by now, it must have settled in her entire blood."

"Have you gone mad? How much slander would it incur, have you ever thought? Pay some extra fees to some doctor and bring him home."

"I am not mad. Instead, you have gone crazy. If something happens to Poonam, then what explanation will I give to my brother and sister-in-law?" Naren, after pushing Savitri off his side, got out quickly from the house.

Everyone now had known what Naren and Savitri had tried to hide since the previous night. As many, people so many rumours. While some sympathised with the orphaned Poonam and callously blamed Savitri and Naren for forcing her to eat poison, the others argued in favour of them, “No, No! The uncle and the aunt are not the only culprits in this. Have you seen this girl? Look at her. She is shrill like the hot chilies, and have you seen her fashion, she would never step out of her house without applying kohl in her eyes.”

The presence of Raghvendra, the tenant boy, and his mysterious overnight disappearance made some suspect some proximity and something hunky-dory between the two. How many such rumours were afloat that had not been known? It was like that loose thread from a sweater. The more it is pulled, the more it is torn.

It was a matter of suicide attempt, so the police had to come. Poonam was not in a conscious state, so the law started questioning Naren and Savitri.

“We did nothing. People did not know how many times this girl had threatened to die after consuming poison. She used to say that she will trap you and die.” Savitri was simultaneously crying and speaking as well.

Naren tried to silence her, but Savitri was too infuriated to calm down. All those family matters would have been solved had they remained hidden but were now made public; Savitri was neither conscious about her honor nor mindful of Poonam’s life. She hardly realised how the washing of the dirty linen in public would affect Poonam’s remaining life.

“Sir, ask her why she had gone into that boy’s room at midnight at two o’clock. If I needed not to scold her what do you expect I should have done; performed a prayer ritual? Had she been my daughter, I would have buried her alive, but I have spared her.”

“Does that mean you don’t consider her your daughter?” The police inspector tried to find clues by hair-splitting investigation but infuriated Savitri could not discern the argument. She spoke before Naren could say anything. "Why should I consider her my daughter? Has she ever considered us her own, and my children as her siblings? No! Never! She has always been concerned about herself."

"You shut up, Savitri, let me talk", in the end, Naren was forced to shout at her loudly.

"Why shouldn't I speak? Had you openly spoken since the beginning, today we would have been spared from this slander and becoming the laughing-stock for the world. When it was time to speak, you were sitting tight-lipped and now you are asking me to shut up."

Savitri was not ready to listen to anyone. Naren wished to slap her to silence her. There was no violence in the family sacraments, which he followed, nor was there any taint of violence in his nature.

Poonam had not regained consciousness until late at night. An army of journalists from several newspapers had gathered at the police station and the hospital. While some of them tried to take the statement of Naren, others were diligently seeking and recording Savitri's version. Naren was silent, Naren was hushed, but Savitri? Her comments had provided a lot of spice to the reporters.

It was a coincidence that Ambuj had been to the hospital to visit some of his acquaintances. While returning, he had gone to meet the Chief Medical Officer. While sitting in his room he heard the chaotic sounds from outside, which had started emerging.

"Why would have this girl tried to kill herself by consuming poison? From what his aunt is saying, it seems that there has been some blooper. It is silly, it is an immature age, and maybe she has done something immoral, indecent."

He had heard only one side. If the girl would also says something, then the situation would get crystallised.

While Ambuj was pondering over the situation's different possibilities, the doctor apprised him that the girl had regained consciousness. The constant recurrence had been, "I wanted to study, but my aunt did not let me study further. My uncle also listened to her and they both wanted to marry me off to a man whose first wife is dead, and he has a child also."

Poonam did not say anything more than this, but presence of a boy in the entire episode was evident from the version screamingly presented by Savitri. It might have been matter of a love affair between both, which is why this girl had attempted suicide.

The police quickly found Raghvendra, the third angle of the story. He told the whole story without any hiccups.

"Poonam showed interest in studying; I was just helping her, nothing else. Sir, I am a student, don't drag me into it. My career will be ruined." He bowed his head with folded hands.

After asking a few more questions, the police released Raghvendra. They had perceived the veracity of his words.

Poonam remained in the hospital for three days. Although, she had been in excellent fettle, the incident's anxiety, despite everything, was evident on her face. When she was about to be discharged from the hospital, the administrative staff called for Naren and Savitri.

"I will not go into that house, these people will marry me and get rid of me, and I want to study, want to be something in life."

"Are we happy with you? Keeping you with us, you defamed us in the entire neighbourhood, what else is left," Savitri started howling loudly.

"Where will she go? We will discharge it from the hospital today." The doctor was confused.

She could be accommodated in some women's hostel or an *ashram*, and then the *ashram* run by Ambuj came to their notice and Poonam was sent there.

Savitri breathed a sigh of relief at last, even though for a while, she got rid of Poonam.

Ambuj, to provide Poonam a shelter in his *ashram*, brought her there and unabatingly extended her hope, a hope for the future; a hope that even she could accomplish her dreams if she wished to. Life is precious and cannot be lost at the altar of petty issues. Life should be sacrificed for a greater purpose, but if someone, hurt by everyday troubles, wishes to commit suicide, there is no one more cowardly than that person is.

Ambuj emerged as a seraph in Poonam's reclusive life. Poonam was acquainted with her desires; her melancholia at non-accomplishment of her aspirations made her secluded from the rest. Negligent of the tribulations and afflictions, she spotted many other girls and women like her when she reached the *ashram*, she came across women who kept their head above water through self-sustenance. With their diligent productiveness, they had accomplished that level where they could ruminate about increasing the *ashram's* income. Those women in the *ashram* persevered with an extraordinary reverence for Ambuj. Reaching *ashram* with Ambuj was the beginning of a new lease of life for Poonam. Fate had tapped at her door, and fortune had afforded her another possibility. Ambuj benevolently introduced her to everyone one by one, quietly leaving behind her odious past and attempted suicide. The *ashram* had certain conduct norms, and Ambuj trained Poonam on multiple aspects of life. The story of grief and pain of the *ashram* women was a mammoth epical tale of suffering.

A woman, victim of her husband's atrocities, supported

by neither her mother nor her in-laws, was eventually abandoned in the cruel world. Then, some girls, tormented by their parents had found refugee in the *ashram*. Ambuj had given support to everyone in this *ashram*.

A girl, who was Poonam's own age, lived in the same *ashram* for the last four to five years. Her parents were also alive, and there were other siblings too. Her story was exceedingly bizarre.

At a barely adolescent age of fourteen, she had to exact a heavy toll for an unessential blunder. A callow boy from the neighbourhood fully-fledged concomitant since childhood; seduced her and drove her away with him.

When the parents came to know about it, they were exasperated in disgust. Although, they had made an official complaint with the police department, ironically, they were not ready to accept her in their house when apprehended. After being liberated from the police custody, they kicked her out of their house when she returned home. Neither the boy's family accepted her nor did her own family members give a positive response to her.

When she fatefully tossed back at the police station, a kind-hearted police officer sent her to Ambuj's *ashram*. Ever since she had arrived there, she had become proficient in the art of pickle making and had mastered the making of poppadum. She was skilled at knitting such warm sweaters that they would be sold hands-on in the winter season.

Poonam felt good to come here, or just to say that Poonam had experienced spiritual peace by coming here. When she learned the story of each individual, she realised that her grief was nothing in comparison.

Comprehending those women, who had been living there and perceiving their wretchedness, she had forgotten her anguish. These women possessed tremendous will power. Even after so much agony and pain, they all had a passion for surviving. They had found the support to move forward, in the guise of Ambuj.

Everyone looked happy. These women suffered much in their lives with no visibility of the traces of sorrow. For the first time, Poonam had come face-to-face with the life's veracity and contemplated how imprudent she had been to have attempted suicide for the little adversity.

□

Seven

Poonam's new life had begun. A new ray of hope had sprung. As per her inclination, Ambuj enrolled her in a nursing school for the upcoming academic session.

Poonam was academically brilliant and promptly became engrossed in her studies. Ambuj used to inquire in between from her about her academic progress. Poonam had completed her nursing training within two years.

Meanwhile, neither her uncle nor aunt cared to know about her, nor did Poonam cared for them. Savitri's behaviour had not been good with her, but for that, she too had been guilty to a certain extent, but Naren? He had been showering a lot of love on her since her childhood. Moreover, why Naren had never missed her, nor had Poonam ever missed her uncle.

However, it was not so in reality. At the slightest mention of Poonam in the house, Savitri would speak against her in disgust. Naren would remember her as a small girl, who had lost her parents as a child, and his dying mother had handed over Poonam to Naren.

Did he perform his duty properly? What explanation could he ever tender to the souls of his brother, sister-in-law, and his mother"? If ever a whirlwind of questions arose in his mind, he would start walking towards the *ashram*. Still, after he got the news of Poonam accomplishing her education further, he was delighted. He would think, "What if his visits to the *ashram* and his meetings with Poonam would become the sordid reason for her being sent back home, and then she would have again become a victim of Savitri's ire," and preferred to remain quiet.

Getting a job was not easy but with the help of Ambuj, Poonam got a job in a private hospital. The salary was not high, but she could easily meet her *own* expenses, while living in the *ashram*. By the way, the ashram's rule was that when any member start earning, he she would have to pay a part of her earnings to the *ashram* so that the *ashram's* expenses would continue and the members too realised their responsibilities. The *ashram* had got many girls married and established them in their respective families. Ambuj deserved all the credit for his diligent work.

"Sir, I need your help." Poonam asked Ambuj one day when he entered the *ashram*.

"Yes, yes, tell."

"Sir, I want to ask my uncle and aunt for my share." Ambuj was shocked for a moment to listen to Poonam.

It is good to ask for the right, but with this bitterness. "But Poonam..."

"Sir, this is my right. My father has a share in that house and shop. After his demise, I have the right on his share."

"Poonam, it's a good thing to ask for your rights, but it's not okay to do it with so much of bitterness. I'll send someone with you talk to your uncle and aunt compassionately."

"Sir, you do not know them. They will not agree easily." "Poonam, don't say like this. After all, they have risen you since childhood."

Ambuj did not like Poonam's words. However, Poonam's aunt was wrong. She had probably abused the minor child. It must have had an impact on her. Still, those people were Poonam's elders and they had looked after her and raised her. When children commit mistakes, parents scold them, so what if her uncle and aunt had scolded her. Poonam was wrong in asking for her share in the property in this way.

It was not sure how much Poonam was influenced by Ambuj's explanation. Although, she had nodded as if she had understood everything, she was not mollified by his logic. How could she easily spare her uncle and aunt? They had viciously jerked from her right to education. They had pinched away her childhood and had captured her father's share in the property comfortably. Ambuj could not successfully fritter away those negative ideas and deleterious thoughts from her mind completely.

Heeding to Poonam's repeated pleas, one day, Ambuj sent one of his employees home with Poonam. However, he was exceedingly indifferent to whatever Poonam wanted to convey to her uncle and aunt. Anyway, Poonam was not legally wrong that she also possessed a right in her paternal property.

Savitri was over and done with that unfortunate incident, removed it from her memory and Poonam had been dead for her. When she saw Poonam in the courtyard of their house after a long span of two years, her heart started beating fast.

"I want to talk to both of you. Call uncle too."

"What do you want to talk about? Aren't you appeased after having defamed us in the whole locality and the entire society? Haven't calmed down yet? Why have you come here again?" Savitri was appallingly incensed at meeting her after a long time.

"You call him. I will leave in a while. I have an urgent matter to resolve with him. If you refuse to talk, you will get a court notice." Poonam straightaway threatened her.

By the most simplistic reasoning, Poonam's firmness

was threatening. The presence of the person, who had accompanied her, was browbeating to Savitri, who stood there shell-shocked, pondering over the impending doom, the menacing slap of the legal notice that she had threatened to serve. To avoid any further ruckus, Savitri thought it appropriate to call her husband.

Naren experienced a mixed bag of joy and surprise, comprehending that after all, Poonam probably had been missing her home after two years, and most likely, the warmth through time had thawed the frozen ice.

Poonam had become more confident after being in the *ashram*, and ever since she had been working, she had become financially independent; her confidence slowly propagated into self-esteem. The protection and the support of an influential person like Ambuj made her enthusing self-assured. The arrogance emanating since her childhood days with the overpowering love of her grandmother and uncle, though slowly diminished with time-lapse, began to lift its head again.

"We wanted to marry her off, but she has not allowed us to be with any face to show. She has defamed us in the entire neighbourhood. Savitri was crying out her grief in front of that employee."

Poonam turned her face and ignored whatever she had said. She remembered her house where she had been born. However, she hardly remembered much about her parents, but she loved her grandmother the most and remembered her aunt's excesses. Right from her childhood, Poonam had been her uncle and aunt's children's babysitter; her aunt would get her to accomplish the daily chores at home, punish her for even the slightest mistake, and would get her off from school whenever she wished. All these things started to emerge like a movie on Poonam's memory board. Her heart woke up to all the bitterness.

Among all this nostalgia galore, she remembered Raghvendra as well. There was some tenant in that room, but this time it was not a boy but a girl. So far, Poonam had not understood whether Raghvendra really had some feelings for her or he was terrified after he got the drift of her aunt's fury. If Raghvendra really had nothing in his mind, then Poonam felt ashamed of the entire state of affairs about how she was willing to elope with him that night without thinking about any consequences.

Suddenly, Poonam's thinking ended with her uncle entering the house.

"Your uncle has come. Now talk." Her aunt narrating the anecdote from the past years for so long sat down silently on one side.

Uncle had arrived. On seeing Poonam, his mixed bag of expressions of surprise and cautiousness emerged on his face, but on second thought, he became normal, or instead, he tried to look normal. He thought that Poonam has come home after two years; she would hug him as soon as she would see him. However, his thought remained contained within him only. Far from hugging him, indifferent Poonam refrained from even basic reverential courtesies. She instead opened up her conversation with her uncle in a short and clear monotone sans any emotion, "I want a share in this house, I want my rights, if you don't give, then I will go to court." Poonam's words had made her voice appear sharper.

Savitri's face appeared reddened and inflamed with anger. Poonam, the little shrimp of a girl, was standing tall with all confidence to confront and confound her of the magnitude of her grievous mistake that she had made. She was about to say something strident when her husband stopped her with a gesture.

Naren had not even imagined that Poonam, who had never coveted to visit home again in the last two years, will once again stand in front of them. However, they were not much aware of Poonam's activities but were acquainted a tad. They were correspondingly aware that after her nursing training, she was employed in a private hospital.

They had been under the impression that since Poonam was happy in her own world, she had probably visited them with intent to share the ecstasy of her success with the family. What if she had instead apologised for the mistake she had made. Probably, they had nursed the misnomer indeed considering if she apologised, they might have forgotten her, but certainly would not have allowed her to leave the house instead. Whatever Savitri would say would still have convinced her. Nevertheless, whatever she had said, he had not even imagined it in his dreams.

Circumstances were challenging and sensitive too, so he handled the matter thoughtfully.

"No need to go to court, daughter. We had to marry you. We had to spend that cost also. Now you may get married on your own. Therefore, take your share." There was intense pain in uncle's voice with a pinch of humour.

After heeding his assurance, Poonam's attitude slackened off, and the person who had come along with her had started feeling comfortable. He had thought that there would be a fight, quarrel, debate and he would have to meditate but nothing happened there.

"Then, okay, do the partition." Poonam said victoriously.

Three rooms, a kitchen, and a small courtyard were all in the house's name. Now there was a problem of how to divide it into two parts. The shop was also small. Why two parts, it was less space for a shop. How should it be divided now?

"Daughter, tell me, how to divide it? We will do as you wish." Uncle asked calmly.

Poonam could not say anything. She had come to ask for her share with a big attitude but she did not know how to divide it.

Poonam came back saying that she would be back after some days and then tell.

Poonam returned to the *ashram* like a victorious lioness but she did not realise what she lost in this victory. She had not expected that the matter would be resolved effortlessly. She had expected good behaviour from the uncle, but her aunt would positively respond to the whole episode with such uncommunicativeness, she had not imagined.

Poonam was caught on the wrong foot, as she hardly possessed an idea of the possibility of any viable plan for apportioning the property. When she failed to comprehend the precise blueprint, she decided to seek guidance from Ambuj.

Ambuj was not sure of her plan. She was appalled by her demand. Her discourteous demeanor still proffered her the privilege to decide her disposal in the impending property dispute circumstances.

"No, Sir. I can't live with them even for a single moment. They will get me married to an old man and will not even let me do a job," was all she said. Poonam wished to fly high and marriage at that moment appeared as the most notable drawback.

Ambuj's curiosity knew no bounds at Poonam's aggression to demand her rights. On the other hand, was she doing with an intention to retaliate? Ambuj, who had predominantly deliberated over retroverting to society, slipped in her attempt to grasp the extent to which a person can go for furnishing selfish interest, was not sure what would Poonam do when she acquires the property rights? What would be her next step?

Poonam was not sure about her rights and her duties. Moreover, pecuniary benefits reigned supreme. "I will give my portion on rent. In this way, my income will increase."

Ambuj objectively suggested that she take some money instead every month rather than take the house's share. "This will be fine for you."

Poonam nodded in affirmation. She had seized upon the sagacious perspective of Ambuj. If she would get a share in the house and shop, what would she do with that? She lived by herself. The hassle of finding the tenants, monthly collection of rent was more cumbersome than acquiring the property. She was resolved to the idea of taking money from her uncle instead of the property.

His employee accompanying Poonam to her uncle and aunt's house apprised Ambuj of what transpired there. Actually, he wanted to know whether they had accepted, those demands that had been raised by Poonam willingly or not.

"No sir, Poonam's uncle is a very gentle person. He did not even allow Poonam to speak again."

After listening to him, something ringed in Ambuj's mind; so far, whatever he had heard from Poonam was the only real but was unaware of the other side's truth. Was it possible that Poonam's fact was semi-truth? Could Poonam be held responsible? What had been considered an aunt's abuse could have been her aunt's efforts to convince her husband. Ambuj remembered that Poonam was lying unconscious in the hospital when her uncle and aunt abandoned her and left.

Until now, Ambuj had held Poonam's uncle and aunt responsible for everything, but after this incident, he had started feeling that Poonam's temperament must have been somewhere insolent too.

Whatever Poonam had desired, it transpired precisely the same way. Although, the uncle's shop did not generate much income, he honestly revealed the exact payment. Whatever rent he received for the room, he honestly blabbed it out. Hence, it was decided that the uncle would contribute four thousand rupees every month to Poonam. The uncle silently accepted this proposal without any hesitation. Although, it was a challenging proposition for him, as his income had not been very exalted and he possessed a financial burden to cater to the rudiments of two school- going children of his own.

Her aunt purred in retaliation, but her uncle had silenced her.

"Had my brother been alive, even then, our share would have been halved?" He explained to Savitri. Savitri had brusquely fallen silent, jettisoning Poonam perpetually from her reminiscence.

However, Poonam was happy about this proliferation in monthly income; simultaneously, the flight of her imagination had correspondingly amplified nourishing the wish to forge ahead in life.

Few more years had passed. Poonam proceeded with her studies and simultaneously with her career. She nourished her aspirations and was prompted to take a flight. If ever, she watched for anything, it was for prospective feasibility. She had been executing efforts, and Ambuj became her facilitator in all this.

Everything had been going on pretty well. Everybody was trying with a will to live. As Poonam grew older, Ambuj directed the *ashram's* director to look for a proper match for Poonam, but she never agreed to it. As long as she had not achieved good in life and until she had not realised something meaningful, she had no plans to get married, nor in her life had the fabled prince appeared as she had heard through stories from her grandmother.

□

Eight

Everything was going normal. Ramnathji and his wife were pleased with the progress of their son. Now Ramnathji started diverting his attention from trade and engaged in the Lord's remembrance and public service.

Ambuj and Varsha's two lovely daughters were a means of recreation for the grandmother. Varsha was contented. She had embellished the whole house.

However, perchance God had a different outlook. Providence and circumstances sometimes wreak havoc on the human reverie. A human being has the potential to do anything but cannot evade his destiny. One such incident had stacked a heap of sorrows on this contented family, which had shaken everyone.

Ambuj and Varsha had gone out of the city to attend a wedding ceremony. Their daughters had exams around the corner, so they had refused to accompany them and stayed at home with their grandparents.

Ambuj had a scheduled meeting to attend for the next day, so he decided to start back from there in the middle of the night itself. Varsha was apprehensive about leaving at one o'clock in the middle of the night. En route, their travel was a rugged forest of approximately two to three kilometers, where many incidents had taken place. Nevertheless, Ambuj had to return, so he had taken the security staff along.

"Don't panic Varsha, I do not know how many times I have travelled this route."

Despite Ambuj's assurance and patience, Varsha's phobia had not diminished, as she sulked within. She was amazed at her feebleness of her mind. She had never been so weak earlier. Ambuj used to stay out many times for work and would come late at night. She remained awake and would wait for him but had never experienced such an emotional state earlier. Nevertheless, why was she getting so scared that day, she could not comprehend.

They started from there, while she secretly evoked divine benevolence within. More than half the route had been crossed; they had even crossed that dreaded dense forest that had created a mental state of fright for Varsha.

"We have come out of the forest safely. You were pathetically terrified," when Ambuj quipped, Varsha smiled. However, destiny had approved of some other plans.

Even though they had successfully come out of the scare of danger that Varsha had expressed, imminent disaster had been waiting for them.

In that terrible blackness, the bedazzling fiery headlight from the vehicles coming from the opposite direction would screen the driver's vision for a moment. He would slow down his vehicle and take it out from the side. He had been employed with Ambuj for several years, possessed certain qualities like efficiency in driving, patience, and would tender immediate apologies for his every smallest mistake.

Nevertheless, at that unfortunate hour, even the most skilled person commits a mistake. The battered driver failed to slow down his car at a hairpin turn when the glaring truck approached him from the opposite direction and could not comprehend the tractor-trolley laden with iron rods, which followed the truck. The front portion of the car rammed into the trolley. The security personnel sitting to the left side and Varsha had died on the spot, and the driver and Ambuj had been badly injured and lay unconscious. Ambuj did not even know that Varsha had left his hand forever that had been his firm support. In the darkness of the night, no one could come to know about the accident immediately.

The parents had been waiting for them. Ambuj had apprised them of their return the same day even though it would be late in the night. Janaki would wink for sleep and would rise up from her slumber with a rude shake as if some kind of premonition had set in. It was four o'clock in the morning. When Ramnathji could no longer take it, he called the police. They immediately became active, and every police station en route was informed. Then they could come across the site of the accident at around five in the morning.

Ambuj was sent to the hospital in a hurry, and Varsha's dead body was brought home. Varsha had been holding Ambuj's hand even when she breathed her last. The police had to try hard to disentangle Varsha's cold, stiff palm from Ambuj's palm. Unaware of all this, Ambuj was in the hospital battling for life.

When the body of Varsha was brought home, there was a furore in the house. Both the daughters had been continuously crying and were in bad shape. Many people had thronged to their home. It appeared as if the entire city had swamped there. People present at that moment had been blubbering. In the professional span of so many years, Ambuj may not have earned much money like the one his father did. Still, he had won people's hearts that many people got to their feet to the occasion when the moment demanded, and his earning was visible that day. As far as it could be seen, only men and women wiping their eyes could be seen. There was as much crowd in the hospital as many groups were present at home. Anyone who heard about the terrible accident had come running in support.

Ambuj's body was heavily bleeding after lying injured for a long time. He needed blood immediately. When people came to know about this, there emerged a long queue of blood donors. Everyone had been competing that the blood flowing in his body could somehow save Ambuj's life.

Owing to the iron-filled tractor, Varsha's body had become mangled, but some divine miracle had saved Ambuj even from a single scratch on his face; instead, his calm, balsamic face still appeared as if smiling. Varsha's dead body was decorated like a bride for her last journey and the sobbing changed into an intense cry. There was an outcry all around. What kind of a disaster had broken loose on divine Ambuj was in everyone's mind. Unblessed Ambuj had never done any wrong to anyone even by mistake, why had those excesses of unfortunate incidents occurred to him? Some people believed it to be the upshot of deeds of previous births; others considered it the will of God.

When the elder daughter Tuhina lighted Varsha's pyre at the cremation ground, the atmosphere once again became inconsolable. Even fortitudinous Ramnathji could not repress his tears and cry bitterly. It was for the first time anyone had witness tears in that iron man's eyes.

Varsha had been absolved of her pain that very moment, but what about Ambuj? Even after three days and two surgeries, he had been struggling and, his dismal condition continued to persist.

Incidentally, Poonam was also a nurse in the same hospital. She shivered at the sight of Ambuj when he was brought there in the hospital in that condition. She pleaded with the hospital administration to get her duty attached to Ambuj.

People were busy praying, while doctors were struggling with the treatment. It was the effect of these prayers that the doctors could successfully bring back Ambuj from death's jaws. His bodily wounds had slowly started recuperating; still, he had been mentally unstable. He would begin to speak anything anytime and fail to recognise anyone.

Although his parents were with him, his children were with him, he could not see Varsha. His eyes would frantically search for her in the whole room and when she could not be seen, he would inquire from them about her whereabouts. His mother would somehow hold back her tears and would tell him that she too was instead injured like him.

"Is she so injured that I can't even meet her?"

No one had the answer to the question and, hence, would maintain utter silence on that.

"First, you be fine, and then we will take you to her." Although Janaki had said to console him, she had to exert her full power to prevent her tears, which were at the tips of her eyes, from flowing rapidly.

The wheel of time turned slightly, while Ambuj's condition was slowly and steadily restoring to normal, but he still was not in the condition of suffering some more traumas. The absence of Varsha would have aggravated his agony further. Soon, he started realising as if everyone had been chipping away from his questions and that he started feeling that there was something that is not right.

"Poonam, tell me how is Varsha? Why is nobody telling me about her?" When Ambuj asked Poonam with a childlike curiosity, Poonam's eyes welled up, but she was not allowed to shed tears at such a precarious moment. Poonam made an excuse for work to turn her face away. "Am I asking something? What has happened to Varsha?"

Shaking Poonam violently by her shoulders, Ambuj asked in a somewhat sharper tone.

Poonam had been holding his hand while she condescended how she should respond to Ambuj's query regarding Varsha. A sharp wave of pain seeped into her vein. She kept sitting there unmoved with Ambuj's hand in her palms for a short time before she suddenly rose from there and started fixing the stuff lying in the room just like that. Ambuj failed to comprehend what had happened to Poonam suddenly. She had left the room on the pretext of bringing some medicine. As soon as she came out of the room, a burst of tears held back for a long time slackened out, alleviating the mental pressure caused by them. When she returned to the room, Ambuj was in a deep sleep.

After spending almost two months in the hospital, Ambuj had returned home. Two months passed like two centuries had passed. It appeared as if he had immersed the entire pain of a lifespan in those two months. The nonexistence of Varsha had replenished that pain, but he was scarcely conscious that the tremendous pain had been nevertheless in the offing for him. Along with the healing of the physical wounds, the soreness and the pain were also diminishing, but what about the pain inflicting him mentally.

"Would Varsha be at home or in the hospital?" he asked himself.

The horrific accident that had ruptured his bone rib, what would have that accident done to Varsha? Whether she too is struggling like me in some hospital, room...He thought to himself within.

"No, no, not like me." He got scared the moment that thought came to his mind. His muscles' condition had not yet been strong enough that he could sit and get up without any assistance for the next few months. The doctor had even refused to grant him medical permission to go home, but Ambuj did not agree to their consensus. He had bandages all over his body, there had been a plaster on his legs, but despite all those sufferings, Ambuj also was suffering from a mental worry that he could not move without support. That was the reason that it had become mandatory to employ a nurse for help.

Everyone had been eagerly waiting for Ambuj, for he was coming home after months in the hospital. His parents and daughters had attended him at the hospital and accompanied him back home, while the entire brigade of servants in his house eagerly waiting for their boss to come home.

Janaki wanted to take Ambuj, who had been sitting in a wheelchair, first to her prayer room. It was not wrong either. She never forgot to remember God even in moments of pious pleasures, and for the last two months, all her time had been spent only in the worship of God and in the hospital, while supervising the medical care for Ambuj.

However, what happened thereafter? As soon as Ambuj entered the worship room, his eyes fell on the idols and photographs installed there. He appeared shell-shocked for a moment and then tears started flowing from his eyes and his body started shivering. Seeing that condition of Ambuj, they all got scared. People, who had been working tirelessly, since morning, with the rising sun, for the arrival of Ambuj at home forgot that there had been a garlanded picture of Varsha in the prayer room, along with the photographs of other ancestors. Ambuj had understood where Varsha had been to, during his stay at the hospital. What had all the people been hiding from him all these days? The truth had to be revealed one day but in this form, nobody had thought about this. He felt like crying. It had been unbelievable for him that Varsha had left her and gone forever.

Memories of Varsha lay scattered in every corner of the house. Whither Ambuj would look, he could see Varsha standing there. It felt like an essential part of his body had been separated from him forever. How would he live without Varsha, and why would he live and live for whom? What had been left in his life after her demise? He kept looking for the answers day and night.

"Son, be patient, Varsha is not alive and we all have to bear this pain. Any amount of babbling and moaning will not bring her back. You have to live now for her daughters," his mother would explain. She had been rightly saying. She would console him to feel presence of Varsha by looking at his daughters, Tuhina and Trishna.

He would remember that terrible day, and the discomfort of Varsha. Varsha would be generally patient; however, she was very restless that night. In any case, she was not keen to undertake traveling on that gloomy night. Wish! Ambuj had just listened to her, then that accident perhaps would not have occurred.

Seeing condition of Ambuj, both Janaki and Ramnathji would shed poignant tears. Ambuj, while lying on the bed, would blankly stare at the ceiling, in the void, heedless of what might have been raging in his head.

"Mother, I made a mistake. A terrible mistake occurred. If I had listened to Varsha that night, she would have been among us today." Ambuj would repeatedly recall that ill- fated night and would get restless. He could not even capture one last glimpse of her face that would heighten his grief and suffering.

Impressed by Poonam's services exquisiteness, while in hospital, Janaki had brought Poonam home to take care of

Ambuj. Poonam herself wanted the same arrangement. Her wish had been granted, as she had desired. She would have got any other job but she received the excellent opportunity to serve the person who had been instrumental in changing her life. The memories related to Varsha had been strewn around Ambuj and her absence from the house engulfed him in depression. At such a time, Poonam had many challenges. Ambuj needed not just physical help but mental as well.

The wounds caused by accident could have been cured one day but the scars inflicted on the mind by sudden death of Varsha could not ever be filled.

Although Poonam was much younger than Ambuj, he would become smaller when depression would set in and disturb him. Sometimes she had to handle him like a small child. Poonam would undergo an ordeal, when in a state of anger, he would try to remove the bandages wrapped on his body. Her training and nursing experience were being tested now and Poonam was trying hard to pass in it.

Poonam alone had to work very had in Ambuj service. Ambuj needed support round the clock. The fatigue on Poonam's face was enough to tell everything.

If Ambuj remained fine at night and could sleep peacefully, Poonam would also get a chance to blink her eyes, but if Ambuj's restlessness increased, she would sometimes remain sleepless all through the night.

Janaki's timeworn physique was not proficient enough so that she could have helped Ambuj.

It was only a week after he had come home when Ambuj's restlessness had increased one night. Ramnathji, Janaki, and the two children were sleeping each in their rooms. Tired of all day's work, the household servants were also profoundly engrossed in a deep sleep in their rooms.

Poonam lay down on the plank on one corner in the

room; sleep had just started knocking her eyes when the sound of Ambuj's moaning had swept away the respite from the eyes.

Poonam immediately woke up from her slumber, but she could not ascertain whether Ambuj was in a state of deep sleep or in an unconscious state. Poonam realised the intensity of his pain by the sound of Ambuj's moaning. When she touched Ambuj's forehead, she realised it was burning like hot ember.

Poonam's touch stirred Ambuj's body. He slowly opened his eyes, which appeared red inflamed as if it was blood, which had emerged in the eyes. In the night bulb light, when Poonam looked into Ambuj's eyes, they seemed like burning coal.

For a while, Ambuj kept staring at Poonam, and then in a huff of passion, he grasped Poonam's two hands in his clammy hands.

"Where did Varsha go? You know how upset I am. Promise me that you will not go anywhere leaving me behind." Ambuj closed his eyes with these words, which had emerged out in a blissful tone. There was a sense of peace in place of pain on his face. Poonam's palms continued to sweat in Ambuj's warm hands throughout the night. Poonam could not separate her hands even after Ambuj fell asleep deeply.

Janaki, who had woken up at five in the morning, came to Ambuj's room when she found Poonam sitting on a chair. Her head was on Ambuj's bed, and she had been sleeping deeply.

Moved by affection, she caressed Poonam's head with her hand waking her up from her sleep. Ambuj's hand was still resting on her arm.

"Sir's health at night ...I did not wish to wake you up,

while you were sleeping." She said, while drenching her dry throat, gently stroking and separating her arm from Ambuj's hand.

Janaki perceived Poonam's nervousness as expected, but she felt that taking care of Ambuj was not possible for Poonam alone, for she would get tired by working all day long and then also at night.

She thought that she would ask Sukanya to help Poonam.

Gradually, Poonam had mingled with everyone in the house. One more thing, by which Poonam was impressed was its luxury, living standard, and its glory, which she had seen for the first time. Poonam had been visiting the house many times earlier as well but only from outside. However, when she stayed in their home for nursing Ambuj, she got the chance to realise its opulence from inside. For the first time in childhood, the story of the palace that she had heard from the grandmother's mouth had come to life; it would be like a prince's palace. Why would her grandmother have imagined such a castle for him? That apart, if her parents were alive, would they have been able to provide her such a palace? Many questions would repeatedly emerge in her mind.

Janaki also treated her more like a member of the house than like a nurse. Ambuj slowly started to look like her friend instead of her mentor, which was the need of the hour. Ambuj felt healthy, and his wounds also started healing, but how could anyone heal the wounds and remove the scars that had affected him mentally? Although all the members of the family and Poonam had tried tirelessly for that to occur, the emptiness, which had emerged into Ambuj's life, was not so easy to be bridged.

□

Nine

Sukanya lived in the outhouse of the same bungalow. Even after having lost a lot in her life, she was satisfied with their family's propinquity.

When Sukanya's mother had died after a prolonged illness, she was only four years old. Her father had been an ordinary Hindi teacher in a private school and would fetch a standard salary. The capital that he had accumulated had been spent in his wife's treatment, leading him onto head over heels in debt. Looking at Sukanya's age, many people had advised him of a second marriage, but the word 'half step' had so ingrained his mind that he disagreed. From household chores to looking after little Sukanya, the entire responsibility had now fallen on his head. He could somehow feed her, but while her mother was alive, she would braid her beautiful oily hair and decorate them with ribbon flowers. Although, after her demise it seemed like a problem, still, her father had not contemplated re-marriage. He had been firm in his words.

Sukanya would go to school with him and come back home with him after the school closed. He would reheat the food prepared in the morning, and the food's odor would satisfy both their appetites. Bearing in mind the house's situation getting helter-skelter and the condition of his beloved daughter Sukanya, the apple of his eye, he felt the absence of a homemaker. Finally, he employed an aged widow, who had no one in the world her for the housework work. Sukanya would call her Amma; Masterji addressed her as his sister. Many people would gossip and ask Masterji to explain it to Masterji, "Why did you keep the woman of another house in your house." Still, Masterji had turned a deaf ear as if he had put cotton in his ears and had obstructed unbecoming voices.

A few days after Amma entered their house, the condition of house and Sukanya had changed drastically. Masterji had become confident on the home front, but his limited income and head-on debt had preempted his days and night's rest and sleep. With every passing day, he would cringe, which would augment his mental burden.

Being a Hindi teacher, he could never come across any other opportunity to earn an extra income. Anyway, who would have taken Hindi tuition? Yet, he could manage to get the task of schooling a few spoiled brats from the affluent families at their house. The famous adage, "As will be food, so will be the mind" would not have been promulgated by our ancestors just for the sake of it. It can, thus be easily understood why children from poor background, who are devoid of a comfortable life, get mature early in life.

The rich fathers do not possess any time but engaged to earn more and more money, while the rich mothers enjoyed making and remolding new ornamented jewellery entrusting the child to the servants' care. These unprincipled children would winkle out liberty to offend Masterji on instances in such a situation. Generally, his costume and a long plait hanging from above the head would be a matter of ridicule for them. Nevertheless, Masterji would bear all the humiliation of insult without any wrinkle.

However, the sad days had still not been over. Sukanya had grown up into a fourteen-year-old ninth-grader; her beauty proportional to her age with good features like a tall physique with a chubby face, twisted nose and talking eyes it would fascinate everyone and anyone.

Sukanya had been moulded into a beautiful disciplined girl with Amma's unconditional love and discipline at home and father's canopy in the school.

However, one night, Masterji suffered a sharp pain in his chest and felt as if someone had gripped his heart. His breath was heavy enough to leave his body, and it was difficult to call someone for help rather who would have Amma called for helping them at the unearthly hour of one o'clock at midnight of the waning fortnight moon in the lunar calendar. Sometimes Masterji would restlessly hold the chest and roam around, and sometimes, he would lie idle.

"He has suffered a heart attack. Had you brought him to the hospital then itself, we could probably have done something, but we are trying still, but...," said the doctor making both Amma and Sukanya desperate.

After two hours, the doctors reported that Masterji was dead. Amma could not believe that God could be so cruel to Sukanya and would do injustice to her.

With this, Amma remembered her fate. She was married at the age of sixteen and after becoming, a widow at the age of seventeen, Amma had returned to her maternal home. Her father had already died, and she was dependent on her three sons and daughters-in-law. Amma's coming back to that house had been unacceptable even to the brothers and their wives, but they preferred to remain quiet out of public ignominy and shame. She would patiently tolerate the ridicule of her sisters-in-law for the sake of her mother while she had been still alive, but soon lost her power of patience after her demise as their atrocities grew up more.

The elder brother, who had some affection for her, but due to fear of his wife, could hardly profess his love for her openly, advised her to shift to a nearby temple.

"Keep the temple clean. Two-three more such women, the *mahant* of the temple and one or two small priests also stay there. You can receive your share from whatever offerings the temple would receive, which would be enough for your sustenance."

After that, she shifted to the temple with her belongings. After accomplishing daily chores of cleaning and maintaining the temple every morning and evening, she remained engrossed in singing God's psalms and prayers. She was liberated from the abuses that she had been subjected to at home and felt, as if she had achieved the aim of her life by procuring a chance to serve the Almighty God. However, her world of illusion soon busted, and her peace, religion, and faith appeared nothing more than just a hoax. One night, she rose from bed in a state of utter shock, as she could feel an unfamiliar touch on her body. However, she could not identify the face in the murky darkness, but she could discern from the voice of that person which had not been unfamiliar, to her, who he was.

"*Mahantji* is that you! Why are you here right now?"

"I can go anywhere anytime; I am the owner of this place."

"The owner of this place is God; we are all here to serve him." She wished to tell him but could not speak from her mouth. In a state of the scare of the unknown, she sat with shrunk feet rolled up.

She had known what that touch meant. After all, she had enjoyed marital bliss and had spent a year with her husband. After that, she somehow managed to save herself from the vultures-like ravenous eyes of men who considered her to be abandoned, but "Oh my God! Such behaviour is a great disaster in your court." She thought to herself.

"I'll scream." She somehow managed to speak.

"So scream as much as you can, no one will listen to you, I am going today but one day you will have to be mine. If you agree on your own, it will be fine, or else..." and he disappeared somewhere in the dark.

Amma had been devastated and had stayed up all night with her legs shrunk up and folded.

"Is your health fine today? You look dull today." After seeing her distempered, the other woman residing in the temple had inquired. She was around ten years older than her and had been living in that temple's premises for the last twelve-thirteen years.

"Yes, it's fine." She replied in a sullen tone. "Did the *mahant* come to you?"

Amma was shocked beyond limit when she heard her question. How has she known about it? She had not spoken to anyone about the incident. She indulged in self-remorse whenever she thought about the entire episode and blamed herself for being responsible for his outrageousness.

Since her childhood, she had been hearing that if a man does or says something voluptuous, then it is the woman's fault. If she is restrained, no one can dare, and, thus, is accused of causing a man to indulge in such misdemean our. "He does the same with everyone." Seeing the question mark in their eyes, she blurted out herself.

"What to do? It is our helplessness. Everything has to be endured. Here there is one, and if you get out from here, then there are ten. You tell me, is this not better than the rest? That has been a new parameter of defenselessness."

However, Amma did not tolerate this state of defenselessness, immediately left, leaving her bundle of clothes, and ran away. She met her elder brother in the field outside the village.

"Kill me, chop me, and bury me in the field here, but I will not go back to the temple."

It has been a mystery whether her brother understood anything or not but certainly did not insist her going back. Three brothers had a meeting with each other.

"We are mostly outside our houses; our wives will not let her live in peace. Why not make a small hut in a field a little away from our home, where she will self-sustain herself?" It was her elder brother, who only gave such a piece of advice.

Since then, Amma had been spending her days peacefully in the same hut. Incidentally, Masterji had been a resident of this village and had known Amma's pain from close quarters. For him, there could not have been a better option. With this, Amma's woes had ended, but then she had a new responsibility.

Amma had stumbled a lot in her life, but had decided that she would not let Sukanya's fate be like that of hers. If her father desired to provide her with education and make her financially independent, she would have to do it.

"But how?" These disturbing questions had been confronting her. Masterji had been a private school teacher, where there was no provision of a pension, nor was there any assurance of any capital or wealth.

He had some money in his compulsory fund that she had already received. The school authorities had waived off Sukanya's fees, but that was not the only expense. The bigger issue was from where other costs like the rent of the house, food, etc., would be met?

Amma did not give up. Masterji had deposited some amount in the bank account in Sukanya's name. She had picked up additional household jobs for extra income and had started cleaning, cooking in three to four houses. Although, Sukanya did not like this, she had been helpless. They had now embarked on life's vehicle.

Sukanya had completed her tenth, her twelfth, and has currently been an undergraduate science student pursuing her B.Sc. from a college. Amma had secured a job to take care of children and prepare food in a house, where both husband and wife would leave home to work in an office. It had been a better and more convenient arrangement than wandering in three to four places, whereas, after coming back from the college, Sukanya would provide coaching to small children in her neighbourhood.

Sukanya had excelled in her graduation exam and wished to undertake a training course to become a qualified teacher, but concurrently Amma's health had started deteriorating. She had a constant cough, and she had avoided going to a doctor.

"What has happened to my daughter; why she was worried so much? I am wonderful, and this cough is an inseperable disease of old age. It will end at my death only." Her cough was the reason, or something else had been, but the couple with whom Amma had been working had removed her from work. After many persuasions, Amma had agreed to accompany Sukanya to the hospital, and the X-Ray report indicated what Sukanya had been suspecting right from the beginning.

"Amma, now you relax. You have raised me for so many years. Now, it's my turn."

However, Amma would not like to sit in peace and if it was nothing else, she would start doing household work.

"Nothing will happen to me. I will not leave this world until I don't marry you off and settle you down." Amma would start laughing to avoid the situation when Sukanya would interrupt.

Sukanya had cured Amma's suffering from the fatal illness and had rescued her from the clutch of imminent death. However, when the moment of death is destined, then who can evade it? Amma had fallen due to a vehicle's collision, while fetching vegetables from the market, and then could never rise again.

Sukanya was all alone in this whole world. She could not come out of this shock for several days. There were many memories associated with Amma in every corner of the house. Although, she was not her blood relation, they built up this relationship to be considered much more than that. Even her mother would not have done the same for her, as Amma did for her.

After her marriage, Amma had considered the house of the in-laws as her home, but then that could not become her house for a long time. When she had come back to her parents' house, they had alienated her, and when she had entered their home, even then the misfortune had not left the chase. After the death of Masterji, she had to go from one house to the other, as domestic help, but after Sukanya had completed her studies and work, it would have been a harbinger of good fortune. However, she could not survive to experience happy moments.

Sukanya had also completed her post-graduation, while she had been battling depression. She had started applying for a job and providing coaching to the kids in the neighbourhood, but it had not been so easy, and then someone introduced her to Ambuj. None could decipher what Ambuj observed in Sukanya, but he had brought her home instead of keeping her in the *ashram*.

Sukanya had picked up her luggage and had shifted to

their outhouse. Ambuj had assigned her the responsibility of both his daughters. Elder daughter Tuhina had been then six, and the younger Trishna was four years old. She had been looking after Ambuj's both daughters' studies and other small tasks. The soft-tempered Sukanya would mind her own business and preferred living in the outhouse life of this bungalow, which she found was far safer than the outside world. No one knows how many people would have started coming closer to young Sukanya, who had no one in this world, on the pretext of becoming her guardians, but Sukanya felt completely safe there.

Six years have passed since then. Sukanya had become an aunt to the little girls, friend to Varsha and the daughter of Janaki and Ramnathji, and had made the outhouse of that house her permanent residence.

"How long will our daughter serve us, now it is our solemn responsibility to find a suitable match for you and settle you in your own family?" When Janaki reiterated, the emotions on Sukanya's face appeared many times and went. Sukanya had been a simple, artless girl devoid of any apparent mannerisms and ornate style of talking.

"Amma, I don't want to get married. I have to be with you forever." Sukanya had spoken her mind while she looked down.

Sukanya was the need of the children and Janaki. They suppressed the idea of her marriage, which could have created a void in the house. Hence, the matter of her marriage continued to be postponed. The possibility of Sukanya herself taking any decision regarding her marriage did not arise. Not many men tried to enter her life. After all, how many people did she have a chance to meet? When her father died, she was left with Amma. It had been then she realised how many people tried to trespass, and after she had shifted to Ambuj's outhouse, her world had been limited to that place. Whenever she had to go out too sometimes Varsha and sometimes, Janaki would accompany her. Sukanya had developed immense faith in the whole family that sometimes both the girls would go out with her. The thunder stroke that had struck to that house had jolted her severely. Although, Varsha had been her mistress, she always considered Sukanya to be her younger sister. Sukanya, who had been far from being garrulous, had become more taciturn. There had been a vast expanse of reticence spread all over the house.

Moreover, Sukanya appeared to Janaki as a solution to all the problems of Poonam. Yes, she had been thinking of Sukanya. Sukanya, who had known the house well, could have become Poonam's helping hand.

"But she is not a nurse, how can she...?" Poonam's responded as if someone had entered unauthorised inside her sovereign domain.

"My dear daughter, it is not obligatory to be a nurse to possess a helpful frame of mind. We have known Sukanya for over many years; qualities that this girl possesses are found one in a million. She will help you a lot."

Poonam had remained quiet at Janaki's logic, but she was not happy by Sukanya's arrival.

Nevertheless, why had she been feeling like that? After all, why? What had been his relationship with Ambuj, from that house?

She had entered that house for the first time. She had seen the splendour of that house for the first time. Her childhood memories of the magnificence and majesty of the palatial life and the princes' stories narrated by her grandmother enlivened in her memory. The bungalow was the prince's palace, but why would her grandmother have imagined such a castle for her. Had her parents been alive, would they have provided her with such a court of dreams? A slight groan emerged from her mouth.

Although, she might not become the owner of that palace, she certainly possessed the complete authority to serve its master, which she had been accomplishing with utmost honesty. Still, Sukanya had made a dent in that.

"Have you ever cared for a patient?" She had thrown a direct question to Sukanya

"When Amma had fallen ill, then I had looked after her, there had not been any such opportunity ..."

"Okay, okay, I'll teach you. I have undertaken a methodical training of nursing." Although, Sukanya was much older than she was, the materialistic feeling of being more significant than Sukanya had emerged from her professional training.

Since, there were two of them, their work and time had been divided that had lightened Poonam's workload, but her mental burden had amplified in an equivalent proportion. Sukanya and Poonam had been together for some time so that Sukanya could acquire to operate the initial state of affairs from Poonam.

Ambuj had been mentally indignant, bodily hurt, and disabled even in doing his work. Being a trained nurse, Poonam had been helping Ambuj without any hesitation, but Sukanya had no such experience. Although, she had been living in the house and had been a part of Ambuj's family for the last so many years, she even used to talk to Ambuj only about work, when it would be urgent. Poonam had often rebuked her badly. It seemed as if Poonam had become her rival and wished to let her down in any case.

□

Ten

Sukanya was staying in the outhouse and Poonam in a room adjacent to Ambuj's room. So that not much inconvenience was caused to Sukanya, Janaki asked her to keep in Poonam's room.

At first, the tending services intended for Ambuj had been divided, and then it was the room that was shared in between the two women. Poonam groaned at this grievance, but what she could say, for the house had not belonged to her, she had herself been there for the sake of Ambuj. She was soaked in envy towards Sukanya from top to bottom. Her desire to stay very close to Ambuj and mentally close to his family members had become very strong. For this, he would wholeheartedly serve Ambuj. Whenever she would get the opportunity, she would get engaged in doing something or the other for Janaki and Ramnathji, and sometimes she would enter the kitchen and start helping those who would be working there.

"You are never tired, whenever I see you, you are engaged in some work or the other," Janaki asked Poonam out of love.

"I like to work." She bowed her head in obeisance and ogled secretly at Sukanya from the corner of her eyes.

There was no emotion on Sukanya's face. She had been silently looking at the clock needle to remove the thermometer from Ambuj's mouth.

Poonam would try to mingle with both daughters as well, but after their mother and household members, if they had been connected to someone, it was Sukanya. However, Varsha had been more of a friend to her daughters than a mother had, but whenever the children would wish to get any desire accomplished from their mother, they would approach Sukanya for her support to reach her. A growing-up girl child's friendly mother can always protect her from any untoward incident and opt precisely for the accurate course. Varsha had been well aware of this obligatory duty of a mother. Owing to Varsha's wisdom, both her daughters had been through their adolescence with grace.

No one can fill the void created by their mother's untimely departure, yet both the girls were very attached to Sukanya. Whenever Sukanya got spare time, she would sit with them and ask them about her school. Although, all family members were now close to Poonam, she could not fathom what was going on in both daughters' hearts, which would further infuriate Poonam. Sukanya would become the victim of her frustrating ire.

"In what condition have you kept the room; you do not even know how to live?"

In confusion, Sukanya had left her wet towel on the bed.

When she had just come out of there, she had heard the sound of something falling from Ambuj's room. Ambuj was trying to take water with his hands stretched out when the glass fell. Poonam had not been there when that happened. Sukanya wanted to retort, but she preferred to remain silent. She had a habit of speaking less and often would mind her own business, but at the same time, she had not been so foolish that she would not understand the meaning of what Poonam had said.

Sukanya's presence all around her would be cankerous

in Poonam's discernments, which even she also understood. Henceforth, she would use that room to the minimum; after all, she had her own room.

It had been four days that there had been a new ruckus. Poonam had not been feeling well that night, so Sukanya stayed with Ambuj. In the morning, she apprised Poonam about Ambuj's condition and went to her room. In a short while, children had to go to school, so she gave them breakfast. She was responsible for getting them ready and sending them to school. The children were close with Sukanya that they were cheek by jowls with her so much that they would not listen to anybody other than Sukanya.

After taking a bath, she immediately moved towards the children. The children had taken their breakfast when a domestic servant came and informed them that Ambuj had fallen from the bed. Sukanya ran towards Ambuj's room, leaving the children on the dining table. She saw two or three people were trying to lift Ambuj onto the bed, and Ramnathji, Janaki and Poonam had been standing all around surrounding Ambuj's bed; the feeling of pain was visible on Ambuj's face. The exeruciating pain was affecting his senses.

In a scuffle, they had even called a doctor.

"You should have taken care of him. How did all this happen?" The doctor asked while he gave pain-relieving injections to Ambuj.

Several pairs of eyes turned to Sukanya. Why? Sukanya could not grasp.

"Where had you been, my daughter, see what has happened to Ambuj?" Janaki tried to appear as humble as possible with her tenor, but her son's pain could not hide her bitterness.

"I had gone to get the children ready for the school... I

had told Poonam..." Sukanya stumbled while she completed the matter.

"Me!" Poonam jumped with surprise making Sukanya more surprised than her.

She had explained to her, but why had she been refusing? Had she made any mistake?

"If Poonam had not come here immediately, what would have happened? Take care ahead." Janaki said ending the matter right there.

Sukanya looked at Poonam. There had been no emotion on her face. Her attention was more towards Ambuj, so is it her mistake? Her head bowed down in shame.

This incident deepened Poonam's infiltration in that house. That was what Poonam had wished. Initially, Poonam, who had been standing behind Sukanya, gave no importance to her after the incident. However, there was a friendly conversation between the two, thereafter.

"Are you fond of writing a diary?"

Sukanya queried Poonam after she had watched her writing routinely for a few days.

"Yes, it feels good to write something, on a day-to-day routine, what have I learned, what has been good, what has been bad, I write everything." Poonam replied keeping an eye on the diary.

"Good habit, but I wonder if anyone can write honestly about himself/herself. It's is one thing to recognise your shortcomings, and to accept them is another thing."

"You are right, but you hesitate when someone else reads it. I am not such a great personality that someone can print a book out of it and bring it to everyone," Poonam laughed out loudly.

At that juncture, Ambuj called out and Sukanya walked towards him.

"You know Sukanya, my aunt had left no stone unturned to do me harm, but May God bless Ambujji who showed me the way."

Poonam would often narrate to Sukanya the so-called atrocities committed by her aunt. At the same time, she would never miss pinpointing the affection that Ambuj had for her. She would claim when Ambuj was in the flutter of pain, how her presence would provide him relief.

What beautiful word 'affection' is! Her father loved her; her mother loved her; and Ambuj's parents loved her. While using Ambuj's name, the style with which Poonam had blinked her eyelids and the facial expressions that had emerged with the word 'affection,' defined it's meaning in some other way.

Sukanya had felt it too. Even Ambuj used to call Poonam for all his work. So, is it possible that a bond of affection had been taking a birth between Ambuj and Poonam? This question would often arise in Sukanya's mind, but she would herself outrightly reject the idea the next moment. Poonam was a trained nurse, she had been to serve the sick man, and then Ambujji had done a lot for her. In a situation like that, an emotional connection is normal thing to happen. As such, her emotional connection was not even less, but more than Ambuj, she was connected with the other members of the family, especially both the daughters. It was Poonam there right in the house who appeared going through a mental turmoil within herself. Ambuj's condition was improving slowly but steadily. He could walk a few steps by himself, but he could not walk normally without support.

In any case, it was also confirmed to Poonam that after some time, Ambuj would not need a nurse. Then? Then what? She questioned herself, pondering over the fact that she would have to return to her hospital and rejoin her duties and would have to live in a room adjacent to it, and would have to leave that beautiful mansion.

"Can't I live in this mansion forever?" A thought flashed through her mind.

"But how?" Another query emerged in her heart along with its rejoinder.

"Is it possible?" It felt as if Poonam was standing in front of the mirror, questioning herself.

"Yes, why not?" If she tries even a little, then it can be possible. "Ambuj's parents are impressed by her service and I have supported Ambuj in a state of loneliness and deep depression."

"But it is your duty; you are her a nurse."

"So, what happened? Don't I have a right to proceed ahead?

"Like this?"

"Yes, in this way only." She ended this question and answer session here.

Many girls like Poonam are working as nurses in private hospitals. The reputed hospitals of the city treat the well-known people of the town also here. In such a situation, it was not uncommon to be introduced to people, in a of some extra money. Even seriously, ill people had to go to their house. There is no shortage of money in some families but with no time to serve the sick. It was not uncommon for nurses to go to such homes for jobs, but it was definitely not normal to think weird like dreaming of living in the same world, not forgetting it, wishing to live in it permanently. Poonam was also a victim of this uncommon mistake. Her grandmother had wished a 'dream palace' for her, when she was a kid. She kept the dream alive in a corner of her mind and now has become active to get her dream realised by thinking of becoming Ambuj's wife.

Six months had passed since Ambuj came home from the hospital; his physical condition improved as was expected. He started dealing with business-related work at home and so the time of Poonam's return seemed to be approaching. He no more needed a nurse, and then Sukanya was still there at home.

"My dear, we have become indebted to you for a lifetime. Had you not been there...." Janaki gently patted Poonam's head with her hands.

"I am indebted to Ambujji. Had he not have helped me on time, then how would I have been able to serve them?"

Poonam finally left the house after taking many gifts. "Now you have all the responsibility to take care of

Ambujji." Sukanya could not decipher whether those parting words uttered by Poonam while leaving, encompassed a natural concern or she had been jealous.

□

Eleven

Life was proceeding steadily but not at a grasping pace. A strange silence had spread throughout the house. Ambuj was performing all his work from home and would sometimes go to office but like a machine-powered object. Neither he nor his two daughters had recovered from the agony of Varsha succumbing to the calamitous collision. An unusual death-like quietude gripped the entire house, and the old parents were devastated by the tragedy and its sequel progression. The loyal entourage of servants was conscious about smiling even among themselves. Tuhina and Trishna had matured untimely with the wobbling doom of unusual seclusion from liveliness, happiness and vitality. After school, they assembled near their father remembering when they both galloped to report school things to.

"I am older. First, I will tell mom." If Tuhina claimed her right to be the firstborn, then Trishna was no less.

"I'm younger, and the first chance is given to the younger ones."

"You two change your clothes first and have something after that; I will listen to both of you leisurely." Judicious Varsha would resolve those petty conflicts promptly.

After Varsha's demise, Tuhina and Trishna were left with no enthusiasm to recount anything, nor would Ambuj be interested in listening to their cute little anecdotes. Ambuj was attentive to his fatherly engagements and tried to manifest his reliance on his daughters' interrogatories. Still, his mental vacuity had been so profound that none could bridge it in any way.

Whenever he would overhear the communication between Varsha and the two girls, he would often be reminded of the mother bird's chirping with the two young birdies in their nest. The bond connecting the mother to her offspring is a strong connection. The enlightened people have determined the perception of differences between parents and children as a "generation gap." Although, the friendliness and bonding between parents and children existed there, there was no obligation for any before-mentioned concept and its definition at their home.

However, Sukanya felt those changes in the conduct of girls. She indeed attempted to fulfill the vacuity that emerged in children's subconscious, but it was improbable for her to supplant the mother.

"What is this, Sukanya? You haven't been taking care of Ambujji. See, how weak he has become in all these days." Poonam demurred Sukanya when she revisited the family after a week. Poonam mounted high her luminous wings on two ostentatious expressions, 'caring' and 'nursing'.

Sukanya neither verbalised nor clarified, but she was familiar with Poonam, who attempted to humiliate her many times even earlier. Still, she could never decipher the rationalisation behind her slur.

"Ambujji has become very weak."

Poonam had not petitioned her grievance to Sukanya directly but had formulated her solicitude towards Ambuj.

"What should I do, he keeps working quietly all day long, he neither talks to anyone nor laughs, what had been my son earlier and don't know what has happened to him now?" Janaki lamented.

Self-confident Poonam re-assuredly cautioned her of the dangerous consequences, if she abstained from complying, "He needs a partner who can understand his pain, can share his pain. Otherwise, he would be suffocated and would gradually slide into depression."

"Yes, you are right. However, where should we find such a partner for him? Varsha had not even, for a moment, made him feel anything wanting in his life; no one can replace her in Ambuj's life." Janaki said, with tears gushing down spontaneously from her eyes, but she let them flow. The mental vexation lightened somewhat.

"You must find a good partner for him, though the absence of Varsha can never be substituted by any other woman in life, but still..." She had gingerly enunciated her concern concealed in her mind.

"Whatever you have said is right, but will Ambuj be ready? Moreover, it has not been a year even that Varsha left us."

When has the clock ceased ticking for anyone? Since time is at its premium, so why would it have paused for Ambuj? Slowly the first two years surpassed everything else but not the grief, and there was no noticeable and evident change in Ambuj's life. Sukanya, with her indispensable existence in the house and Poonam becoming a member of the house, even though she was not living in that house, were the few significant changes.

Ambuj also started operating his office even when he had a little but persisting pain in his left leg.

One day, when Ambuj went to his office to complete some indeterminate official documents and records, Poonam appeared there. She frequently visited their house but he was astonished to observe her in the office. He, with an apparent outburst, "You, here?"

Aggressive Poonam would never disregard her selfish interests, especially, when they were at a stake. She wistfully blurted out, "I could not meet you at home, so I thought I would come here and ask about your well-being." "Why? My mother didn't inform you anything?" Ambuj had inherited his propriety of response from Janaki. His gentle smile indicated his awareness that his mother admired Poonam. Janaki was convinced that Poonam had nursed Ambuj when he had been suffering from mental trauma and when his appalling state necessitated nursing care the most. She drew him out of the rigmarole of depression, and somehow Ambuj had been appreciative of her. Poonam authoritatively punched the statement, "Your mother wasn't complaining", revealing her conviction.

Janaki was wearied of Ambuj for being insensitive and neglectfully misled in his grief. Poonam reiterated Janaki's concern, "You don't take care of yourself, don't talk to anyone. And you just keep to yourself."

"I had been the same before; what difference has occurred now?"

"No. You had not been like this before; even I had been watching you." As an entrepreneur and a committed social worker, Poonam deemed Ambuj an advantageous prospect for her but something obstructed her. She aspired to state something but her voice smothered within.

"You want to say something?" Ambuj had realised her condition.

"Yes, why don't you get married?" She spoke immediately.

Ambuj was shocked, for he had not expected such a suggestion from Poonam. In the last year, many people had suggested this sympathetically to him. Some connected his remarriage to proper upbringing of children. Others gave reason for his own life, but the memories of Varsha were so deeply rooted within him that there was no scope for any other prospect. What right did he possess to ruin someone else's life? How could someone be established in the household, when emotionally he doesn't liquesce for that person? What is the use?

He felt like retaliating bitterly to Poonam's query so that she could not dare suggest any other thing after that, but then he recollected her services rendered to him in his bad days and decided not to. In his moments of illness and depression, Poonam had been his most outstanding support and had stood together with him. She had entered the house as his nurse but had emerged as his friend with her kindness. All these reminiscences forbade him from speaking bitterly in retaliation. He judiciously and facetiously adjourned the entire matter.

"You haven't married even once, and you suggest me my second marriage. It is a total injustice."

Poonam's face had turned red. She had not expected an answer like that. Instead, it also seemed to her that Ambuj would not pay attention to anyone other than her.

When Ambuj returned home late that evening, Janaki had been waiting for him.

"Your daughters are of growing-up age, and there are a hundred complications of this age. They can't confide everything to everyone, and there should be someone as their listener."

"Sukanya is there," Ambuj pretended to remain unknown, despite conjecturing the meaning of mother.

"Sukanya cannot take the place of a mother. Children have considered her more of a governess."

"What is the guarantee that children will accept any new person, who enters their life and would consider her to be their own?" Ambuj expressed his doubts.

"You just say yes, my son. It is my job to find such a girl." Janaki became excited.

"Mother, not the girl, but a woman. Don't take advantage of anyone's helplessness. The one, who would say yes willingly, will do, without any pressure...."

"You know your mother. I will never allow anything bad for anyone." Thousands of lamps of hope illuminated Janaki's face.

"One thing, mother." Janaki choked. What else Ambuj wished to say. She secretly hoped Ambuj, who had agreed for remarriage, should not refuse and that would have extinguished those beads of happiness in one stroke.

"You must introduce her to Tuhina and Trishna, and if something bad happens to them, I will not be able to forgive myself for a lifetime", impassioned Ambuj got emotional.

□

Twelve

The children only needed a mother for a few more ensuing years of adolescence. After that, they too would get engrossed in their own families, leaving Ambuj all alone. Ambuj had been so lonesome and necessitated life-partner more than anybody else had.

Janaki implicitly was conscious of the entire scenario, and it was necessary to address it with children. The children's relationship with their stepmother has been defined implicitly through storytelling, movies and serials that no one can trust this relationship. Janaki had already removed this fear from the mind of Tuhina and Trishna.

Ambuj's acceptance renewed the fresh wave of vigour into Janaki's life. She cried when she hugged her son in gratitude.

A quiet smile enveloped Ambuj's face. "How happy mother is today?" He thought to himself and that was more than sufficient for him.

Mothers are like this—aggrieved even at their children's slightest suffering and exultant at their little joys. A feeling of great sorrow for their children breaks them. When he looked at the exultant happiness on his mother's face, he too felt thrilled.

How sad his parents had been for some time because of him.

Ambuj, all his life, had always possessed a strong mental desire to look after the oppressed people of the society and had ever worked for the grieving people. Even the wealth in millions appeared petty to him in comparison to the slightest joy on their faces. However, it did not occur to him that he could provide happiness to his parents, indeed, with a little effort.

A few days after he had nodded to his mother's plea one afternoon, Ambuj had been sitting with a file when Janaki approached him with a picture and showed it to him.

"This is Anjali. She is not too young for you. It has been some time now, when she lost both her parents. Her father had his own business, now she is managing this business herself. Her father's brothers are there but everyone is occupied with their own family. None discerned, nor did anyone bother that Anjali had to be espoused and married."

"You have consolidated all the data about her as a detective." Ambuj chuckled mischievously.

"It is a question of the children and your future, and then the most important thing is that they should not come under any pressure to accept."

"Have you spoken to the children?" "Son, majorly, you have to affirm it first."

"Mother, you would always like better for me, ask the children formally and familiarize them. I have no problem with that."

Ambuj's apathy had knocked Janaki mentally. What if sometime later, he would remain indifferent to Anjali too.

She removed her dilemma from her mind and walked towards the children's room before Ambuj might change his mind. She wanted to materialize his remarriage with haste, all by herself.

When both sides nodded in affirmation to each other,

Ambuj and Anjali met, children had met Anjali, and everyone fixed the engagement day.

"Mother, what is the need for engagement? It will be fine if the marriage takes place in the presence of limited people of the house." Ambuj was not in favour of any formal ceremony.

"Son, marriage is an important event in one's life. Everyone has aspirations, dreams, tries to remember this day according to their ability. It might be a second marriage for you, but for Anjali, she is becoming a bride for the first time. Why should we impede her wishes?"

"Mother was right," Ambuj thought and then he decided not to interfere anymore.

There had been a series of discussions at home and quite plausibly, Sukanya knew about Ambuj's remarriage plans or the marriage prospect of Anjali for him. She had been a little surprised, as she had convincingly presumed that whenever Ambuj would ever get married, Poonam would be his first choice. Even during his severe depression days, Ambuj was very close to Poonam, and Poonam also made gestures often indicating towards this, but where was Poonam all those days? Sukanya reasoned to herself.

"Poonam! Where are you nowadays? You haven't come home in the last so many days." Coincidentally on the next day, Poonam was there.

"What's the matter, Amma? You seem to be very happy."
"The thing is like this, and if you listen too, you too would be blissfully happy." Janaki's voice had been brimming with enthusiasm.

After Varsha's departure, Poonam had seen Janaki so pleased for the first time.

What could be the reason? While she had been thinking

about the overtly reflected happiness, Janaki called out for Sukanya.

"Sukanya! Bring sweets from inside. See, Poonam has come."

As Poonam picked up a piece of sweet from the dish and put it in her mouth, Janaki told her the reason for her happiness.

"Ambuj has agreed to the marriage, and we have also found the girl for him." That which had been gratifying for Janaki and others, the same information had turned Poonam's taste buds acerbic. The piece of dessert that had filled her mouth with sweetness had turned bitter than the *neem*. She felt as if she was caught in a vicious circle of catch-22.

"Anjali is a very good girl; both children have also met her."

Janaki had been speaking impetuously, oblivious of Poonam's facial expressions. However, Sukanya could see the intense and the waning colours on Poonam's face.

Had Janaki been ignorant about Poonam's emotional state? While she had been serving Ambuj wholeheartedly for so many months, had she just been doing her duty of being a nurse? Poonam thought.

Alien to Poonam's state of mind, Janaki had been busy showing her clothes and ornaments with great enthusiasm. The impact of the beautiful ornaments of more than one designs, the best new designer saris bought from select shops of the city, had consumed Poonam to the extent that a snake of envy sprawled through her mind.

"All these things should have been mine ... these sarees should have been hers." Poonam reflected an anguish.

"Did you like them?" Janaki asked in a motherly voice.
"She is asking as if these had been brought for me," Poonam thought in her mind.

"Is Ambujji at home?" She retorted with a question for a question.

"Yes, he is, but right now resting. You can meet him afterward? You will come in engagement."

"Yes, I have to come."

Sukanya had anticipated the intensity of pain and anguish in Poonam's voice. What had been that Poonam wished to articulate after all?

"This saree is for you; come wearing it that day." Janaki handed over to Poonam a packet that had contained a pink-coloured saree for her.

"Huh! She is giving me this saree as if she was making me her daughter-in-law; I do not want any charities from her." As soon as she reached her room, she threw the sari packet on the bed. Her face had turned red with anger and resentment tears had stopped on her eyelids.

"What has happened to you?" Gunjan was home after her duty. She lived in the same room with her and was startled to observe her condition.

"Ambuj is getting engaged, and his mother has given me this sari for me to wear on that day."

Gunjan could feel the anguish in her voice. Poonam, who had always been addressing Ambuj as Ambujji with respect, that day had forgotten the typical norms of courtesy.

"With whom?"

"There is some Anjali. I served Ambuj for so many months. I have stayed with him in his bad times. He had professed love for me and now when the question of marriage has arisen, he has conveniently removed me from his life like a fly from milk. Do we low have no respect?"

"Why are you getting upset? Talk to Ambujji once. He has a good image in society. Maybe, there is some misunderstanding." Gunjan explained. For many years, she had been living in the same city and had been familiar with Ambuj's family.

"I had a wrong perception! What do you mean? Have I misunderstood anyone? They have used me, made me a part of their family when it was desirable, and..." Poonam had started panting due to excess of anger.

Gunjan kept quiet. Poonam, too, became silent for a while, tried in vain to gulp down her tears, and then started targeting Gunjan.

"You, too, will take their side only. They are big people, even if they do excesses, they will remain clear and clean, stigmas of dishonour are written only in the destiny of the poor, but I will not spare them."

Gunjan did not deem it appropriate to say anything at that point to Poonam, who had been fuming, and when her power of thinking and rationalising had considerably waned.

Poonam strolled across the room for a while before sitting down resignedly in the chair in a state of utter exasperation. Then she descended from the chair and started rambling again. Gunjan had already contemplated that her psychosomatic condition had not been in shape. Without saying anything, she placed a glass of water in front of her. Poonam stared back at her as if she would devour her. However, she took the glass of water from her and emptied it in one breath.

There had been silence in the room for some time. Poonam had propped her head on the chair and kept gawking at the rooftop. To give her company, Gunjan, too, got immersed in her thought sitting on the bed.

"Are you alright, Poonam?" Gunjan had prodded her, while simultaneously breaking the silence.

"Do you think I can be okay? Ambuj has upturned all my

desires. When he needed me, he used to call me a member of the house now, and when I wanted to become a member of the house, they want someone else to want them. What kind of people are they?"

"You tell me just what it is which I lack? Do I not deserve that house? Is a magnificent mansion, luxury, splendour, prosperity not itemised for our destiny? Gunjan, please tell me. Why don't you say something?" While lamenting for her forfeiture, Poonam sat on Gunjan's bed.

Poised Gunjan professed her undaunted friendship to Poonam with the intent to reveal her the appropriate path or what she deemed fit concurrently apprising her of the actuality. "Look, Poonam, I know that your heart is in deep anguish today. You are pained that all of your dreams are falling apart." Gunjan had been well conversant with the standpoint she had to take, giving preference to Poonam and her friendship.

With a calm and solemn gesture, Gunjan continued to tie her talk.

"Don't say anything in an ambiguous mode; speak in a straightforward and clear style. Your philosophy is beyond my comprehension." Poonam again starting fuming while interrupting Gunjan.

"Poonam, it is not a philosophy, it is life's veracity ... fathom it, comprehend it. You always have said that you have felt emotionally involved towards Ambuj's family. It was natural because if we have heart-to-heart tête- à-tête with anyone even for two days, we naturally get predisposed towards that individual and start nourishing an attachment sentiment. However, you have taken care of Ambuj by staying in that house for so many months, but ..."

Gunjan was speaking when Poonam interrupted again. "What the hell?"

"But it is not necessary, Poonam, that the responses that evinced in you for Ambujji, while you had been in that house, the same kind of response should also have germinated in Ambujji?"

Poonam's face had triggered an inquisitorial sentiment after Gunjan had utterred those words.

"Poonam! How much time has passed since that event? Of course, it has been a year for you and us, but in Ambuj's psyche it has been a momentous event for him. Think, Poonam, he lost his wife, and himself struggling with physical and mental trauma and suffering. Your services and gentle behaviour worked to bring them above the vortex of this sorrow, but you could not heal the wounded heart, and you know the reason for that."

"What is it?" Poonam asked in exasperation.

Gunjan reiterated judiciously, "Poonam, the reason for this is not that, Ambujji doesn't wish to recover from that injury. Probably, he wishes to keep the remembrance of Varsha alive every moment in his memories. Her voice still must be resonating in his ears; his body might be shuddering at the feeling of her touch even today. I am sure he must still be seeing a shade of Varsha in his daughters Tuhina and Trishna. He might not have said but must be feeling and must have absorbed that most painful pain in his heart. In such circumstances, a feeling of love must have arisen in his mind towards you, may be not Poonam."

"No Gunjan ...It is not so. I have felt many times that he spoke to me in the love charm."

Poonam said, while clinging to her perspective.

"Don't know Poonam ... this I cannot tell ... and if yes...I think something like this. Suppose it seems to you that Ambuj has not confided in you his real feelings because of hesitation. In that case, you can go to him and confront him, but saying intemperately and thinking inordinately about the matter is wrong."

Gunjan wanted to put in plain words to Poonam, but Poonam had been reluctant to pin her ears back to anyone's advice. She could apprehend only the comfort of a rich palatial mansion that was sliding down from the firm grip of her hands. She had concocted and rustled up a indomitable blueprint to make an entrance into that mansion in any case as Ambuj's wife. She was discerning with eagle-eyed possibility within herself to go to any extent to accomplish her goal from her penalty area. She spoke, "Gunjan, this is not the time for me to think about these things. I have to do something or the other but yes, I will meet Ambuj and I will ask him why he has done this to me?"

Gunjan had realised until then that it would be a futile exercise to make her understand anything, so she, too, stopped. She said to her with a dreary feel, "Whatever you want to think, think, what you want to do, do, but directly I would like to tell you that you should not think of perpetrating any injury on a person who has endowed you a renewed lease of life. Had you have undeniably been enamored by Ambujji, and then you should feel love-bound to be contented in his exuberance. Furthermore, love has to go through the rigour and grind of repudiation many times over. If you wish to remain a member of that house, for that you do not need to become Ambujji's wife. Why not devote your life to them beyond any such aspiration and without being tied to such a relationship? I am coerced into credence that your fondness for Ambujji resides outside him into his splendour, brilliance, and opulence appended with him. Your grandmother created the delusional fantasy, and you are being surrounded by resentment and downheartedness like this one. Oh, you should feel blessed and grateful to Ambujji, who has made you independent."

After saying this, Gunjan covered her face in her sheet and pretended to sleep.

However, Poonam remained unmoved as if no one had said anything to her.

□

Thirteen

Poonam had appeared at ten o'clock in the morning the next day in Ambuj's house as a menace. Her stay in that house for over many years had acquainted her with everyone's routine. She had known their practices on the tip of her fingers like Janaki would be in her prayer room, Ramnathji would be in his room, and Ambuj would be in the study room. Poonam was considered a member of this house, so no one stopped her when she went directly to the study room.

"Congratulations, I have heard that you have agreed to the marriage, and also the relationship confirmed." Poonam spoke sarcastically.

Ambuj immersed in his book's pages that he had been browsing, could not decipher sarcasm in Poonam's comment.

"Hey, Poonam! Thank you. You came after a long time." He lifted his head and looked at Poonam, but her facial expressions appeared tangent to her presentations and indeed not meant to greet. Her face seemed as if stuffed, her blazing red eyes, her trembling hands rested on the table.

"Poonam, is your health fine?" Ambuj panicked after seeing her condition.

"You haven't done well to me rather cheated me." Poonam's voice had been quivering. Ambuj was shocked. What had been that he had not done well? What had been that double-dealing Poonam had been referring to?

"You pretend to be a tremendous social worker, don't you. You have given support and assistance to countless impoverished women, but it's all posturing. You have grabbed gratuitous advantage of my sentiments. After your wife's departure, I kept grinding your ax, and now when the time of your marriage approached, you have preferred to espouse a match from an affluent family." Poonam could not obstruct her tears after that.

Ambuj had started discerning the unmitigated state of affairs in small portions. For some time, he had been grasping the apparent revolutions in Poonam's stances and physical responses. She had always been on the lookout for an evident reason to come in close contiguity to him. Whenever she would visit on a duty call to Ambuj's residence, her attention would be absorbed more in Ambuj and his obligations and hobbies. It had not been that Ambuj had been oblivious to her inappropriate demeanor. Instead, he had perceived it at the outset but did not resist or refute it either for his etiquettes and decorum of behaviour or just for the error of judgment that had landed him in an awkward situation.

Ambuj could not decipher exactly how to respond.

Poonam had been dreadfully fuming at that moment. Had he reacted aggressively, it would have provoked her more. He had been confident that dealing with the issue deftly could only bury the hatchet.

"Poonam, you are much younger, and to be more precise, I have under no circumstances perceived you in any other role than that of my younger sister. Why have you fostered a wrong impression?" In a composed accent, he endeavoured to make her easy with the situation.

However, Poonam had emerged in the form of a bellona.

When Ambuj had attempted to make her comprehend more, she turned out to be more distraught.

"Oh, is that so! So now, you are fantasising about me being your sister. I have surrendered myself completely. Why haven't you dredged up beforehand to tie the *rakhi*? What do you understand of yourself? I will take the wraps off your actual appearance to the whole world." Moreover, she stamped her feet and stomped out in anger.

Ambuj had become traumatized by her aggressive behaviour.

Why had Poonam been comporting herself like that? He had been helping her in every possible manner ever since she had left her uncle's household. He had made efforts to backing Poonam to acquire employment in a large hospital in the city.

He remembered Poonam's initial appearance when she had regained consciousness. She had been shouting at her aunt in foul, abusive language, and her aunt's reaction by the same token had been reckless. While Poonam had been distressed by the fact that she had to move back to her house, her aunt had also not been interested in Poonam's repatriation. Her uncle and aunt had not to wrangle over when they had apportioned the property.

Had Poonam's nature been correspondingly fierce? Had there been any behavioural problem with Poonam that she could not keepup with anyone? This aspect of Poonam's persona had also caught his attention.

Now, it was to be seen what would be Poonam's ensuing action? Had she coveted to rake up a quarrel? On the other hand, had the charge just been her momentary reaction? What would supervene? It had been veiled in the womb of the future.

Despite everything, the engagement ceremony was

solemnised, Poonam did not show up for the commemoration. Janaki was surprised as she asked Sukanya to call Poonam, but her mobile persistently remained switched off.

"Today, she had to go somewhere, today is the day of Ambuj's resuscitation towards life, and the person that had helped him get out of this depression is not here." Janaki had not anticipated her absenteeism.

Nevertheless, Ambuj was assured of her non-attendance. However, he had been apprehensive of transpiring something untoward that would repeatedly haul his attention towards the main gate.

The ceremony was straightened out in all tranquility. Anjali had been happy that she had Ambuj as her life partner and mother-like Janaki as her mother-in-law. Ambuj had been psychologically content that the current association satisfied his daughters and his parents.

Poonam had been neither in the hospital nor at home that day, "Where would she have gone?" Gunjan deliberated. After she retreated from Ambuj's house, there were blended reactions of disgruntlement and irritation on her face.

"If Ambuj can't get married to me, then I will not let him get married to someone else."

"But what happened? You went to meet them, what did he say? "Gunjan was holding her hand, forced Poonam to sit with her.

"What could he say? He just said that he has no such feelings towards me."

"But you used to say that he loved you?" Gunjan could not understand anything.

"Yes, I have proof of this, now see what I will do." Poonam's anger was not calming down in any way.

"What do you want to do?" Gunjan got frightened after seeing Poonam's condition. She was not aware of what had been going on in Poonam's mind. She recollected how Poonam had attempted suicide earlier as well after her aunt had scolded her.

"I will go to the media. I will report it to the police. Then, I will see how you enter into another marriage."

Gunjan panicked after perceiving Poonam's intentions. Ambuj may have been in love with her, but for some reason, he probably cannot get married to her, but in the past, he has provided Poonam ample support. Had he not cooperated with Poonam, then, there would not have been any chance that Poonam could have progressed so far. She should not be so ungrateful, and she explained that to Poonam.

Poonam's eclipsed expressions kept emerging on her face.

"Probably there has been some impact." Gunjan thought. There was peace for two-three days. Neither Poonam raised the issue again, nor Gunjan teased her.

On the day of the engagement, Poonam had left the house in the morning. Any efforts to contact her had been futile. Mentally, Gunjan kept wandering like a nomad throughout the day in fear of something untoward.

She had a duty in the hospital until in the afternoon; after that, she could be relieved. Gunjan catered to her professional responsibilities, but her focus kept hovering somewhere else. Whenever she saw that three or four people gathered at a place and saw them talking, she would drift her ears automatically towards them. Probably, she would hear something about Poonam. Generally, none of the employees, patients, or visitors can keep their phones on a loud ring tone in the hospitals. Gunjan repeatedly looked at her mobile, which she had kept in silent mode in her pocket to ensure if she had not missed any call. Anyhow, there was no communication about Poonam.

Presumably, Poonam might have recuperated from her melancholia, Gunjan thought in a self-explanatory monologue. She could hardly ascertain that it was a dismal lull before the impending storm. Poonam returned late that night to depart from the house early in the morning. She had taken leave from the hospital.

The next day had been just like any other regular day, but it was a moderately altered atmosphere in Ramnathji's house. The wretched murkiness that had daubed the house after the untimely demise of Varsha gave the impression of getting impeccably sunnier and brighter. However, there had been no alteration in anyone's routine.

Ambuj had been in his study room when his mobile rang. There was his lawyer on the other side.

"Ambuj, there is a problem." His lawyer was much older than Ambuj and was like a family member, and their affection was less professional but more devout, like that exists between a father and a son. Ambuj instantly could assume from his voiced tone that though he coveted to articulate but became diffident instead.

"What's the matter, Uncle? You look upset." Ambuj's heartbeats had been racing. He suspected whether the untoward incident that he had been most apprehensive until a day before had probably proven to be true.

His suspicion had rolled out to be accurate. Poonam had accosted and tactfully prepositioned some local women's organisations with their workers to enroll a matter of exploitation against Ambuj.

Ambuj owned a courteous and benign deportment, which had always been ready to help everyone, and the number of well-wishers was not less. On the other hand, there was no shortage of jealous and legal transgressors in the society and environment of professionals, who always weighed Ambuj as a snag in their road to success. He had blocked the market for those people, who would extort money in the name of social organisations from the government and various institutions. People expected their opportunity as fence-sitters to pounce on so that they could imprison Ambuj in their scheme of things. Poonam conveniently became a puppet in the hands of such people. The issue was not small either. How could he be alleged to have involved in any kind of so-called exploitation of the miserable and helpless women for whom he had been working?

There were allegations because of the girl who he supported. He would form a relationship with everyone without any blood relationship. Today, he felt like the wall of every such connection cracking up.

He wished to apply for anticipatory bail. In a short while, the lawyer appeared with some papers. Ambuj signed the papers mechanically. Neither he asked about anything, nor did the lawyer say anything. There was no such thing in that problem that could have been discussed.

"Naresh had come? He did not come to meet me. I know how busy these lawyers are." Ramnathji had seen the lawyer hurrying back.

"Yes, he was in a hurry. He had come to get some important papers signed," Ambuj responded with his head bowed down. He did not dare look at his father's face. Probably he was scared of his experienced father and his sharp vision who he thought could have easily deciphered his nervousness and untruthfulness.

Nevertheless, how long could he have hidden that from the rest of the family members? Even if he had somehow hidden the matter, the next day, it would have been published in the city's local newspapers and would have been the breaking news for them.

However, he would not have to wait for the next day. In a short time, the news spread like wildfire in the whole city. By the time it was afternoon, several women's organisations were shouting slogans against Ambuj outside his house. This house was, until then, a symbol of social prestige and prosperity.

"What is this happening? Why is it so crowded outside and so noisy? What happened after all?" When Janaki heard the noise, she stepped out of her house.

"Nothing, mother, you go inside, I'll look into the matter."

"Why nothing, the voices of slogans against you are coming up to here, and still you say no problem, will someone not tell me what the matter is?" Janaki panicked as the slogans of public ignominy and condemnation amplified by the voices she heard emanating from outside. The more Ambuj attempted to remove her from there, more her curiosity would increase. How could he talk in front of his parents about such an unpleasant affair? In a short time, the entire matter emanated clearer to everyone. While Ambuj and Ramnathji shielded themselves up in profound silence, Janaki was twitchy to bump into Poonam. "Bring that girl in front of me. I will ask her, why did she do this? How lovingly we had kept her in the house like our own daughter." The depth of faith in her son was so deep that she could not deliberate upon an obligation to probe the integrity and the fabrications inherent within it.

"Mother, you stay calm. Everything will be all right. There are no legs of lies. This lie, too, will falter in no time." Ambuj attempted to keep Janaki quiet.

Shortly after, the police removed the crowd from there and controlled the situation, but the spark, buried in the fire ashes that day, became a blaze the next day.

Almost all the city's local newspapers on the next day in the morning had been smeared with this news, but there was an eerie silence in Ambuj's house. Nobody had even touched the newspapers.

In this house, Sukanya was immersed in some other abstraction. She felt Poonam's inclination towards Ambuj more times than one, and Poonam herself indirectly had accepted it in front of Sukanya.

"Was Ambujji too...?" Sukanya thought, "But Ambujji is a lovely man. If that was so, why would he had consented to get married to someone other than Poonam." Having lived in that house for the last so many years that much faith she had on Ambuj.

"If that is not so, then what is that Poonam wants? She owes so much to this house that she wished if she could meet Poonam and talk to her and explain." After constantly pondering over it, Sukanya, on the pretext of going to the market, headed towards Poonam's hostel the next day to discover her locked room, while Poonam was unapproachable.

Gunjan was off to her duty at the hospital. Sukanya went to her.

"She hasn't come home ever since. I was on duty in the morning when she left. Since then, I do not know where is she?" Gunjan's eyes were staring intently downwards.

Whatever Poonam had done, its guilt was visible on Gunjan's face.

"Why are you getting upset? You have not done anything." Sukanya tried to console her.

"I had tried to convince a lot to her. If there was anything like that, then remember his past help and appreciation and leave this thing. I thought it was accepted, but now it is ..."

"Was there anything between Ambujji and Poonam?"

Sukanya asked Gunjan a direct question. She was surprised at the intensity of her problem. It was her habit to talk without any restrictions, but she would never speak in such cases.

"Poonam used to say so." A simple flat answer to the question came to Sukanya's mind also once. Ambuj and Poonam were close to each other when Ambuj needed both physical and mental peal. It was not an unexpected event that Poonam handled him in such situations.

Gunjan got into speculation, ever since Poonam came back from Ramnathji's house, she attempted to retrieve the events till now. However, apart from what Poonam said, she could not recollect anything that she could grasp from Ambuj's side.

"Ambujji never gave her a call. Yes, in the beginning, his mother used to call her on the phone." After stressing her mind, Gunjan was able to tell this much. So is this a story made by Poonam? And if so, how will Ambuj get out of this maze? He did not know what mystical maze was created to trap Ambuj, but Sukanya couldn't understand it. Sukanya, who leads a simple life, could understand only the conspiratorial mind.

Sukanya's suspicion was not incorrect. The police had already given some such evidence that they could not postpone Ambuj's arrest.

The news of his impending arrest had raged like the fire, which would spread in the forest.

People had started gossiping about the shreds of evidence that had been provided by Poonam.

If someone said there is a recorded evidence in the form of a CD of their intimate relationships, the other was convinced about the availability of the recorded conversations between the two. People do not believe many facts about men. They could not think of Ambuj, who could do something like that but preferred to maintain a silence because of the evidence.

Sukanya was shocked. What kind of proofs Poonam had possessed?

How much truth was there in those shreds of evidence?

What was the truth behind those shreds of evidence?

Sukanya had once again become disconcerted. Probably, there had been those weak moments, some emotional weakness or something like that.

Another family associated with Ambuj for the past few days had been the family of Anjali. In a few days from then, Anjali would have become important members of their family. What would be the future of that relationship? Would it be possible to hide that incident from Anjali? In the era of Ambuj's personality and media hyperactivity, how would that be possible?

□

Fourteen

Anjali looked at the newspaper with a sip of tea, as she set her eyes on a news story, one time, twice and multiple times over. She attempted to understand it numerous times; the name, the description, everything matched correspondingly with Ambuj. Since she was in a denial mode, she immediately rubbished it off. Anjali had come across lots of praises for Ambuj, only then she had consented to marry him at this mature age.

Anjali was younger than a brother was and studied management, while living with him in the US when a terrible accident took both their parents' lives. Her father and uncle lived separately in an ancestral mansion-like house. The business was also divided along with other property between the two families. After the parents' death, the son came home for a few days, but he did not endorse the ancestral business compared to a company based in the US. After completing the requisite formalities, he went back abroad. While leaving, he asked Anjali to dispose of the business house and accompany him to the US. Sensitive Anjali was attached emotionally with the house from her childhood. Especially after her parents' sad demise, she could not do so because of the inherent nostalgia of her memories treasured in that house. Her uncle also discursively coveted that Anjali, like her brother, should bequeath the entire company to him but dared not to manifest that opinion after scanning Anjali's sturdiness and firmness.

Progressively, after conjecturing the business's subtleties, Anjali accepted the industry's halters under her administrative charge. Since then, Anjali had never more glanced backward. She promptly doused herself terrifically with her work that she could never retrieve anything different. Never had she yearned for anything, nor had anyone else noticed that Anjali's marriage had to be consummated. Incidentally, there had been none in Anjali's life, who would have swept her off her feet. None could bowl Anjali over; the intention of getting married did not transpire to her either.

She was charmed with her life, or we can say that she could never grasp a chance to be dissatisfied due to excessive busyness. Some senior family members would randomly refer to her marriage, but they never approached her with any proposal, whether suitable or unsuitable.

Her workaholic elder brother would visit her once every year from the US, but his arrival recurrence diminished progressively. After Anjali had been through thirty-five springs of her life, a distant aunt of hers suggested Ambuj's relationship.

Her aunt grinned in exasperation.

"First of all, he is a widower, and he is the father of two daughters. Was there no other proposal left for Anjali?

"Then why haven't you ensured something for her in the preceding years?" Without missing the opportunity, her father's sister rolled up her eyes and had pronounced sarcastically.

However, either of her aunts had failed to impress an eager beaver Anjali. She accepted her determination, even if not everything was appropriate, even if someone kept saying a million times over. Sometimes, she would take business advice from her brother.

Once, she felt like telling her aunt most audibly, then not knowing what, she called her brother.

"Anjali, though it is your affair, I would say that in life, someone or others must be so close that you can share your happiness and sorrow. We don't have to share only sorrows and happiness; if something in life is good, then sharing it makes the mind happier. I have heard about Ambuj that his family is reputed and him too. Rest as you wish."

In this statement of her brother, his indirect approval was directly visible to Anjali. He was not saying anything wrong. After her mother and father's demise, she pushed herself into business and progressively climbed the ladder of success but was lagging in her personal life.

She would receive good wishes for her success in business and celebrating success as well. Still, everything would be mechanised like a rocket that is like an emotionless face as if they were given the command to smile that day. The extent of flattery would be such that she would feel embarrassed and ashamed. She would always look for a person, who, along with her success, could also tell her the faults of her failure. She made powerful fortress retreat around her, the doors of that impregnable fort opened only for Ambuj.

However! Now this news! Ambuj was arrested. Poonam had presented evidence to the police. She kept pondering over her decision whether her decision was wrong. Anjali, who believed in karma, did not have much faith in destiny but the arrest of Ambuj raked her within that perhaps there was no scope of a life partner in her future.

"Can one person have multiple faces?" Anjali asked herself.

It seems like this. Otherwise, one who claims to be a social activist across the city can not be so bleak on the other side.

Two days passed; Anjali had not spoken to anyone in this regard but her aunt, pretending to be her benefactor, did not miss taking a dig at her. She came as a friend, but in the gestures, she made Anjali's heart wrench.

"The father of two daughters was not ashamed while doing so... I already used to say..."

"Nothing has been proved right now, aunt." Anjali stopped her in the middle.

"You may not have read the newspaper precisely. Police possess evidence and all the shreds of evidence are against him. What else remains to be seen and heard?"

"Can't say anything until the crime is proved. Probably, the pieces of evidence are false." Although, Anjali tried to convince her aunt, she could feel the vibrations in her voice. The aunt went on wryly, twisting her mouth, but left

Anjali drowned in the whirlpool of her thoughts.

When she had crossed what is called marriageable age in Indian culture, suddenly this relationship like a star fell from the sky. After the initial reluctance, she accepted it from the heart. On meeting Ambuj, she found him a man of her mental caliber. After his first wife's demise, battling physical disability for a while had broken him, but he possessed the rare ability to rise after falling.

"Is it so important to get married?" The question raked up from within. The reason that emerged strongly for her affirmation for relationship was the answer to her question. "But the relationship that has a rough start this way, what would be the future of that relationship? Maybe, the allegations on Ambuj are true and if he is punished, what will she do then?" When this question arose in her mind, she spoke to her brother.

"It may be a lie, and it may be accurate, but is there a lack of problems in life that she would marry a disputed person and invite another tension?" She had a simplistic inquiry.

Finally, the corresponding decree emerged again.

"This is your life, do it as you see fit." He is right. This life is filled with distress and doesn't lack problems. So, why should a new problem, a fresh concern be invited?

Even if Ambuj somehow would have released on bail, where would be the guarantee that after years of the judicial process, he would be left spotless?

"But what if something happens after marriage?" One more question originated in her mind.

That was a different thing. Troubles keep coming unexpectedly in life, but already known unfortunate incident cannot be gulped.

After many questions and answers, repertoire and analysis, logics and arguments emerging in her mind, Anjali took the decision.

Four days passed once Ambuj's bail application was dismissed, and Anjali was correspondingly watching for the precise moment to convey the message of her decision to Ambuj's house.

The twilight of the evening was deepening. The sun was drowning in its entire ambience. In the grand residence of Ramnathji the empire of the darkness had spread there. As soon as they remembered Ambuj being locked in a stockade cell, they felt like igniting up their home.

Ambuj had been in jail for four days. His bail application was rejected. The court presented some mobile recordings as evidence. Ambuj's family did not know what was there in it.

Nareshji himself was present in the evening. There are

some photos and videos taken on mobile. "They seem to be real, but I have applied for his forensic examination. By the time the report comes, I will have to seek bail based on Ambuj's medical report."

"You do whatever you want, take him out. Here these four days have appeared like four centuries."

"Actually, the law is stringent in such cases. It is an exercise to stop crime against women."

"Has Ambuj committed any crime?" Ramnathji had a question in his mind. Who knows their children more than their parents? Because he tended towards society in childhood, he was sent to America for studies. Even after returning from there, his thinking had not changed. Since then, he had raised the parents' head by his actions, but what has happened now? The charge is so disgusting that they could not even debate it. They had visited their son in jail and appeared in the court on the court hearing day, but it seemed as if everyone's eyes were on them. If there had been two people talking to each other in the corridors, it appeared as if they spoke about them. Many well-wishers rang them up but Ramnathji felt their tone more satiric than concern in their voice. Ambuj, with his hard labour, had left everyone sluggishly dawdling behind. The corresponding opponents had been standing with their heads raised in defiance, watching the spectacle of their equality.

Sukanya was in a dilemma, what she could do for the family. In the hour of grief, in those four days, it had been challenging for everyone. The girls did not realise what, after all, had happened?

Sukanya tried to entertain them somehow by keeping them with her so that any rumour or gossip should not damage the young children's innocent psyche. She did not send children to school in those four days.

"Aunty, why is grandma crying so much? Where did my father go? Why aren't we going to school?" Little Trishna asked many questions at one go.

"My dear, the grandmother is ill, she is hurt, so tears are rolling out automatically, and your father has gone out on a business commitment; he will come back soon." Sukanya tried to convince them, but it felt as if her own words emanated from a deep well. What, if something like that did not occur? What if the charges against Ambuj are proven right? When she looked at the children, her mind shivered. When girls would grow up, people would ask several questions. If they go out, the public slur would not have let them survive. Sukanya felt as if all that she had been imagining had been happening in front of her. Scared and scarred, Sukanya spread out her arms for the children and took them within the fold of her embrace.

She wanted to meet Poonam. She wanted to ask, "Why she desolated the whole family?" However, Poonam was coming to her own house some business organisations had retained her with them. They had been threatening Ambuj's entire family with dire consequences. Perhaps they were also in jeopardy that Poonam should not turn away from her statement later, and they may not lose the opportunity against Ambuj.

Sukanya hurriedly finished all the household work in the night and went to her room, lying on the bed with the intent to sleep, but her troubled mind frequently disturbed her.

"How can I sleep peacefully?" The house had given her a new lease of life, gave her hope to live. Today, the lives of the members of such a place had been surrounded by utter despair. What must be going on? The initial disaster that had rocked their lives was Varsha's sudden demise.

At the same time, Ambujji had been injured physically and mentally. Now when the situation was returning to normalcy, Poonam had caught the disaster in the guise of exploitation. Oh God! Why do you do this? Why does God prick the thorns in their feet of those who walk clearing the thorns from others' lives? Ambujji has taught people to live in a society that had been frustrated, despised, tortured and broken to live life. He has endowed them with fresh energy, taught them its meaning, gave them purpose so that they do not consider their life meaningless.

What is happening in his life today...it is a popular belief that 'what you sow so shall you reap,' but Ambujji did not sow anything that he would have to reap a crop of thorns with this kind of sorrow, and he has been left to grieve like this.

Why is the life of that person who makes the life of every needy happy, so painful today?

Why did the blessings of those thousands not fall on this family?

There had been numerous other such questions that Sukanya kept asking herself or to God.

What could she do at such a time that the circumstances of this house could become a little easy?

Her ideas, emotions kept emanating like the waves in the sea of thoughts and finally, the mind stopped at Poonam.

Poonam, yes! She should reach out to Poonam. Who knows, she might agree if the right picture is shown to her so that she withdraws her case.

While thinking about it, when sleep had caught her eye, she was unaware of. On the pretext of going to the market the next morning, she went to Poonam's hostel to find an answer to her questions.

□

Fifteen

It was Sunday, Sukanya met Gunjan in their hostel room itself.

"Come, Sukanya...." Gunjan said, gesturing to come inside while opening the door.

"How are you, Gunjan?" Sukanya asked. "I'm fine. Is everybody okay at home?"

"Not fine, Gunjan. Where is Poonam?" Sukanya jumped straight to her query.

"I do not know where she is. She has not come to the hostel since that day, nor has she contacted me but Sukanya, everything she did was very wrong. She has hatched a conspiracy with a man who supported her, educated her, secured a job for her, and above all, gave her a sense of belonging. How did she manipulate to bite the hand that feeds you?" Gunjan told Sukanya with a heavy heart.

"Gunjan, the same thing is bothering me even now. To fulfill her aspirations, how can someone stoop so low?"

"Gunjan would share everything with you. What did she say about Ambuj?"

Sukanya told Gunjan for exploring things.

"Yes, Sukanya! She used to say that every day, almost every day; she would talk only about Ambujji and his house. According to her, Ambuj loved her too. She used to say that Ambujji did not like to talk to anyone except Poonam, and maybe she did not like even your presence near him. She wished to get that house at any cost."

Gunjan kept on narrating everything that she had perceptibly known, and Sukanya tried to understand her each word.

After listening to Gunjan, Sukanya asked Gunjan. "Gunjan, I want to ask you for something, will you give?" "From me? What can I give Sukanya?"

"Lend me your support, Gunjan." Sukanya stood up, grabbed Gunjan by her shoulders, and said, "I will explain," Sukanya emphasised each of her words.

"Gunjan, if you wish, then we both together can get relief from these moments of sorrow for Ambujji."

"How Sukanya?" Gunjan questioned.

"First, promise that you will support me." Sukanya put her hand forward.

Gunjan held her hand firmly and said, "Look, Sukanya. Poonam is my best friend, and I have fulfilled every duty of friendship. I tried to make her understand not to mess with that person who gave her life again, but she did not listen to me. However, I have not met Ambujji in person, nor I know much about him; when he is appreciated for his actions in society, respect is automatically generated for that person. Ambujji is an ideal person, Sukanya. I have sincerely done my duty towards my friend, but now I want to rise above all and fulfill the duty towards humanitarianism."

"Thanks, Gunjan! You do not know today about how encouraged I feel after meeting you. My happiness has increased so much. With some mixed sense of hope and despair, I had left home, but you have removed my fear and heightened the light of hope." Sukanya said excitedly.

"We have to help such a person, who has given birth to the good in society."

"Okay, Gunjan, do you think Poonam had some habits that you have felt are different?" Sukanya asked.

"Nothing special. But yes, she had a habit that she did not give up under any circumstances and that was her habit of writing diary."

Sukanya was also aware of this habit of Poonam. Hence, she asked Gunjan, "Can we find some evidence in this cupboard," Gunjan nodded in affirmation and opened the cupboard.

There were some clothes, some books related to nursing and other small items in the cupboard. Sukanya looked back over the books to look for a clue, in the form of a piece of paper, but could find nothing. Sukanya was frustrated when her attention shifted to some clothes, placed at the bottom of the cupboard. When she removed the clothes, she saw some three or four dairies lying there.

"Is she used to writing a diary?" "Yes."

"Does she write all the truth?"

"Yes. Which novel is going to be published on her diary?" Sukanya suddenly remembered this conversation a few days before. There appeared a glow of hope in her eyes, as well as a question.

"Will you find anything in these diaries?"

With the diaries in hand, Sukanya wanted to leave Gunjan.

"Thank you, Gunjan Thank you. You helped me a lot."

"Please don't say thank you, Sukanya. I have promised to support you. I will also go to court with you if need be. You do not worry, everything will be all right." Gunjan reassured Sukanya.

Sukanya returned home with a kind of spiritual satisfaction and a sense of gratitude towards Gunjan.

When Sukanya came back, there was a strange silence in the house. Although, the errie silence had become a part of the house, the silence of that day appeared slightly deeper.

"Anjali has broken off the relationship." Janaki explained the reason in a short sentence.

"Why did Anjaliji do this? Couldn't she wait even for a few days?"

Whom Sukanya could have asked this? Real friends and enemies can be identified in trying moments. Anjali had abandoned her relationship with Ambuj even before the adversity could be done away with.

After invoking the blessing of the Almighty, she started looking at the diaries sequentially.

The three diaries were dated before Ambuj's accident; however, when she picked up the last dairy, her eyes flashed as soon as she saw the date.

She read the diary as a novel from the beginning to the end. As she read it, her eyes widened. There emerged a moment that her eyes were filled with a lot of happiness, words started fading away, and she quickly wiped away the tears so that they do not blur the content of the diary.

When she looked up after going through the diary, she saw the time, it was eleven o'clock in the night. She felt like raising everyone from their beds and make them read what has been written but she avoided it for it had already been late. Although she also knew that sleep had been missing from their eyes for the last many days.

They might have slept or not, but sleep was away from Sukanya's eyes. She kept waiting for the morning and read Poonam's other three diaries as well, only to discover how ambitious she had been and could do anything to fulfill her desires. Sukanya could create a picture of her ambitious persona.

Sukanya could not sleep overnight waiting for the dawn.

Children not had been going to school for the last few days, so Sukanya had no vital commitment for the morning.

"Why are you up so early today?" "Yes, I could not sleep more."

"Yes, who is sleeping in this house these days? That girl had stolen our happiness, rest and sleep; don't know, she is the evil of which birth?" In the morning once again, the reference to the unpleasant incident broke out.

"I have to talk to you, and it would be fine if you can call the lawyer also."

Have to talk in front of a lawyer too. Now, what has happened to Sukanya? Is there going to be another new problem?

"Don't worry, and everything will be good. I have some evidence in hand, which can help Ambujji." Sukanya immediately said after she had read Janaki's facial expressions.

After a while, all the diaries were in front of Nareshji.

"I remembered Poonam was fond of writing a diary. No matter how busy she was, she would take out ten minutes out of her busy schedule. When this thought came to my mind, I took help of her friend Gunjan. I have read those diaries. She has not written anything fictitious. You first take a diary of those days when she was here."

He turned the pages of the diary and looked at Ramnathji, and Janaki stared at him. A ray of hope was emerging in their minds, but there was also a question mark in the restless mind. "Has Sukanya found something that could help them?"

"What is written in it?" Ramnathji almost peeped in the diary. "Hey, let me read first, and then only I will be able to tell." The relationship of friendship always dominated the professional relationship.

"You have done a great job. You have saved the honor of this family." Then looking at Ramnathji, he said.

"I will take these diaries home. I will sit leisurely all day reading them. I hope all is well." While Naresh lifted diaries from the table, he awakened a ray of hope in the hearts of Ambuj's parents, who had become hopeless from all sides.

Janaki looked at Sukanya and wanted to say something but could not utter a word. In a spurt of emotional outburst, she grabbed Sukanya's hands. The language of touch proved to be more potent than words. Sukanya had understood.

☐

Sixteen

The entire room was packed. After all, it was the proceedings of the hearing of the city's most famous case. The noise emanating from the room appeared like the humming bees' sound, and most people expected the court's decision would be cancellation of bail for Ambuj.

Well-wishers of Ambuj waited for a miracle, had heard good about this family for so many years and many families worshiped him.

A worker from an NGO was seated with Poonam in the front row. Her face shone with the emotion of haughtiness. As if she was giving the message that a woman, who is considered weak, can be so powerful.

As soon as the judge entered, there was complete silence in the courtroom. Like the warriors standing in the boxing ring, lawyers from both sides stood face-to-face with all their preparation. Although, Poonam's lawyer was confident of his victory, Nareshji's confidence was disturbing him from within.

The pictures taken on Poonam's mobile were substantial proof, which were evident and narrated the closeness of the relationship between the two.

At the very outset, Nareshji emphasised that Poonam had taken the pictures to draw benefits from Ambuj's condition and blackmail him. At the same time, Poonam and her lawyer were emphasising that she captured the images with mutual consent, and there was a testimony of a flourishing relationship between them.

Many well-wishers' hearts fluttered along with Ramnathji who was present there with the arguments presented by Poonam's lawyer. Poonam's heart also exploded, not in fright but in the hope of a possible win.

Now it was the turn of Nareshji. "My lord, I have some such shreds of evidence that will change the picture of this case." Nareshji's slow and solemn voice echoed in the court. Poonam looked carefully. He had a packet in his hand. "What is there in that packet? What could be the evidence that will falsify my charge." "This diary..."

"Diary! Oh, is that so!" The words naturally emanating out of Poonam's mouth had spontaneously caught the attention of the people sitting around.

"Is there anything special in the diary?" The director of the NGO questioned her aggressively.

Once again, the sound of murmur like the buzzing of bees had spread in the court. The judge stroked the hammer on the table to ensure order and pin-drop silence in the room.

There was silence in the room even before Poonam could utter anything.

Only Nareshji's voice echoed in the room, but there was a volcano-like eruption within Poonam's mind. Once again, she was losing the battle. Why has she been so careless? She knew that every word written in that diary was correct. Her feelings, her desires, her ambitious plans that she had voiced in that diary had started pirouetting in her mind's eyes. She tried to make out a sense from those words, but they abandoned her and ran towards Ambuj.

"What a big house this is, just like a palace. Did the

prince live in a similar palace? Had my grandmother dreamt of such a chateau for me?"

She had written those lines when she had entered the house for the first time.

"Today, Ambujji was very restless. He took Varshaji's name many times in the state of unconsciousness due to high fever. How fortunate was Varsha who found such a loving husband! She had enjoyed both physical and mental happiness."

After some time, she had become jealous of Varsha, who was beyond all the joys and sorrows.

"Ambuj, in his sleep, took my hand in his hands. He kept in that state for a long time. He was blabbering something, but even after trying hard, I could not understand. Like a nurse, we both have touched each other many times, but this experience was amazing."

Poonam had stopped putting the respectful address of 'Ji' with name of Ambuj.

She remembered the day when Janaki had been very upset to see Ambuj's condition after the demise of Varsha. The same evening she had wrote down her emotions in the dairy.

"Ammaji has pain in some corner of her mind that how will Ambuj spend the rest of his life. In gestures, it seems that she wants to get Ambuj married again. Can't I take this place?" It was only after this idea emerged in her mind that she started giving it a proper shape.

"Unknowingly, today, I took a picture of both of us on my mobile. It seems as if two lovers were deeply embraced in love. Wish! It could be possible even when Ambuj is conscious."

Poonam remembers that there was no malice in her

mind, while taking that picture, nor did the idea of its misuse had arisen in even a remote corner of her mind. What she treasured was the unilateral affection that she felt for Ambuj.

However, gradually this love turned into an emotion of jealousy. She would be skeptical of anyone growing closer to Ambuj. The people who would partake in the splendour of that house would become the target of her jealousy. She would compare her childhood after seeing the children of Ambuj. Getting Ambuj had converted into her passion and every word of her diary steered towards that disposition of her mind.

"After the annual ritualistic observation of Varsha's demise, Amma is looking for a proper relationship for Ambuj. Ambuj cannot belong to anyone other than me. This majesty, this amenity is my right, only mine, such a palace will be for me to live and Ambuj is the prince of my dreams." In that eccentricity, she took many pictures on her mobile strewn everywhere. Those pictures became substantial evidence against Ambuj.

Many such things had found mention in her diary that had made it evident that to accomplish anything, Poonam, with her one-sided passion, could go to any extent.

The woman sitting next to her shook her shoulders. Then the words dancing in front of her eyes suddenly appeared from somewhere in the room. Nareshji requested permission to summon her to the witness box.

Poonam's feet felt like tottering as if there was no breathing left. Poonam's haughtiness had been dashed to pieces for venturing to prosecute such a magnanimous personality like Ambuj. The chimera of those so-called feminist organisations that coveted to infect the perfect image of Ambuj had also shattered.

After comprehending everything, the court's judgment come in favour of Ambuj, and the court ordered to register a complaint for cheating and malicious adjurations against Poonam.

A relentless tornado transpired and disbanded. The hurricane did not cause any havoc, but its catastrophic impact was too much on Ambuj's mind.

Ambuj was a brooder, and he additionally cloaked himself in reticence. Janaki and Ramnathji felt as if they had expended Ambuj even after extracting him backward safely. Ambuj was immured in a chamber. After perusing all the court proceedings' specifications, Anjali's brother called on Ambuj, apologised to him, and yearned to reconnect the matrimonial coupling between both. Ambuj was not enthusiastic about this relationship nor was Janaki.

"Then they did not listen to us even once, just heard a one-sided version and resolved to obliterate the matrimonial alliance. Now that everything has gone well, Anjali's family talked about reconnecting a relationship from their side." Unwittingly and convincingly, Janaki's voice became resentful towards them.

Sukanya was among them all. Although, everyone in the house endeared her due to her nature and sagacity of obligation, what she had done to save Ambuj from the apparent slur was extraordinary. It was a lost fortune in which family prestige and everything were at stake and Sukanya was the reason for the victory. Loss of money was not so significant for illustrious family-like Ramnathji's, as was the loss of prestige. Janaki folded her hands in gratitude in front of Sukanya. Sukanya moved forward and grasped her folded hands in her hands.

"You are like a mother to me. Please don't embarrass me."

"You have come as a goddess incarnate for this family." She embraced Sukanya.

Ramnathji laid his hand on her head without saying anything. Expressions of gratitude were visible in his eyes.

□

Seventeen

While Sukanya had been exultant, she was also contented. All that jazz over the years, her small rhythmic movements within the precincts of the house that the family had endured for her, she felt could not be possibly paid back even in many subsequent births. Sukanya's instincts had been raw and straightforward; still, she possessed power of the mind to assay her role in revitalising Ambuj's significant but undifferentiated family. She had rallied round to refurbish its dignity, which had been sufficient for her. She had not forgotten to express her gratitude towards Gunjan.

She would also get angry at Poonam. How ungrateful a living human being can be! A human being, whom God has given heart, could go drastically wide of the mark, could construct blatant fabrications.

Poonam's uncle and aunt had also arrived. Poonam's aunt was unable to shake off the feeling of antagonism against her. She was high on the adrenaline and embarked on the chance to speak against her. She had been becoming eminently vocal, but Naren silenced her. He folded his hands in remorse and compunction to Janaki for his atonement, Poonam's atonement and the atonement of the entire family.

"Now you will have faith in us that we were not off beam. First, in the entire neighbourhood, she brought disgrace to us that because of uncle-aunt's atrocities, the orphan child ate the poison and now this recent infamy." Teary-eyed Naren's throat almost choked in repugnance.

"Being her uncle and aunt, we make an apology to you. She was reprimanded for her actions, but we are not able to get purged of the blasphemy of being her blood relation."

Gradually, everyone tried to forget the horrific incident from the past and kept them engaged in their daily routine. If not anyone could forget that incident, it was Ambuj. First, he was devastated by the untimely demise of Varsha, and then the blasphemy inflicted by Poonam had made his mind like a canker. Ambuj needed an ointment for this canker, even a company of a genuine friend, to whom Ambuj could speak his mind, would have healed his wound.

Intrinsically, though Trishna and Tuhina yearned for Varsha enormously, the scarcity of time and school commitments hardly left them any time to be morose and nostalgic. After the demise of Varsha, Sukanya bestowed love upon and extended her friendliness towards Tuhina and Trishna that they rolled up to her.

One day, it occurred to Janaki what a selfless girl Sukanya was. It was approved that she was rendered unaccompanied in the clogged-up woebegone world and nevertheless not safe for a lonesome girl to survive shorn of any protection. Since she has been residing with them and has entrusted her to them, Janaki thought it would be appropriate if Sukanya could get rid of running errands for their house and enter into matrimony with any qualified person. Janaki had earlier too spoken to her in this regard.

"Why do you want to get me out of here?" Two pearls-like tears had permeated from her soulful eyes, after which Janaki never pestered her.

The children had just returned from school. The pace

of eating at the dinner table was the same as telling the school routine.

"Sister, you shut up. Auntie will listen to me first, "Trishna got frustrated, seeing Tuhina saying her point with galloping speed.

Trishna was the one to speak in an unruffled, exceedingly peaceful and leisurely aloof voice. On the other hand, Tuhina would always be in a hurry, would communicate briskly, subsequently dumping innumerable words within the oral cavity, and doled out with her other responsibilities swiftly as well. Tuhina's quickness would be worth watching whether she would complete her homework or get ready for school in the morning.

"We won't listen to anyone right now. First, both will eat food, rest for a while, complete the homework after getting up, and then a lot of things and sports. If you talk while eating, then the food gets stuck in the throat." Sukanya came to grips with them plausibly and made them eat their lunch uninterrupted.

"Okay, auntie." Both had readily agreed to eat their food unobtrusively while Janaki was carefully watching their activity.

Janaki was left pondering. "How much love and support have these girls received from Sukanya, how attached they have been to her." After the demise of Varsha, Sukanya not only obliterated that feeling where they would have lacked the presence of their mother but also protected them from the terrible mental mess created by the predicament of the outer world. She kept them away from the news flashed in the newspapers and media channels so that their feeble minds are not adversely affected.

Unpredictably, a thought flashed through Janaki's mind,

"Is this possible? Will Sukanya agree to it? And what if Sukanya agrees, will Ambuj...?"

She immediately repressed this idea the instant it emerged in some corner of the mind.

It is a common adage that time is the greatest unguent, which gradually heals even deeper wounds. The same was happening with Ambuj's family. The injury that had been inflicted on them by Poonam had likewise started to heal. Ambuj, too, had endeavored in all conscience to erase that distressing episode from his mind.

It is eternal, it happens. Ambuj started moving out but coveted to keep himself full of activity so that he doesn't have enough spare time to ruminate. Who could ever hide from the deliberating eyes of the mother? The vacuity in his eyes and his withered face were the tell tales.

Embers of the fire buried in some corner of her mind started smoldering ablaze the second it found oxygen.

"How long will Ambuj live such a lonely and cursed life? How many more years would we survive? Tomorrow Tuhina and Trishna will get busy with themselves, then who would be with him?" She confided her intentions in Ramnathji.

"Ambuj and Anjali's relationship could not be consummated because of Poonam. I know Ambuj will not accept it, and even if he agrees, then where will we find such a girl?" She expressed her doubts to Ramnathji.

"I have a girl in mind." Janaki spoke her mind to him.

Ramnathji kept deliberating over it for some time and then uttered peacefully, "Your choice is right. The girl is well educated and polite. Moreover, she is familiar with Ambuj's circumstances, but first, try to be acquainted with the opinions of both. Talk to Ambuj."

•

After dinner, as Ambuj entered his bedroom, Janaki entered his room from behind.

"I wish to talk to you." She sat on the couch nearby.

Janaki's initiative for a discourse had raked up Ambuj's extra-sensory perception. He had comprehended what his mother wished to talk. He had already contemplated how he would apprise his mother about his plans, that he could not bear the pain anymore, that she should refrain from talking to him about it.

Nevertheless, all his planning quashed. Ambuj was surprised by a categorically emphatic point that had been outstretched by his mother. He had never thought about it earlier. He could not come out with any unequivocal rejoinder, although he had been thinking about both daughters. Would it be appropriate for their imminent future? Should he answer the question in affirmation?

However, the next sentence from the mother's mouth also ended this dilemma.

"Mother, don't use your influence; it is not right to have such a relationship in any way."

Ambuj's confession instilled new hope in Janaki's mind of the probability of expected happiness in his life.

Janaki could not sleep the entire night and waited for the sunrise. She repeatedly turned on her bed while disturbing sleepy Ramnathji lying on the other side of the bed. The more she turned, the more he would get angry with Janaki. However, where had Janaki's mind been in her control?

It was morning; it was becoming unbearable for Janaki to spend her time.

"Do the children have to go to school late today?" She asked Sukanya.

"No, mother, they have to go at their own time." Sukanya said, while preparing her breakfast.

"Good! I thought."

"Don't worry, mother, I always know about their time-tables. They will not be late." Sukanya smiled and said.

"Yes, that's why..." Janaki spoke in a deep glottal voice. However, Sukanya had been too busy to pay much attention. "Come and sit with me here. I have to talk to you," Janki seated Sukanya with her as soon as the children left for their school.

"Tell me, mother." Sukanya came and sat on the chair lying in front.

"Look! Daughter! Don't say no! I have come to you with great expectations." She immediately grabbed Sukanya's hands.

"Yes, please speak. I can do anything for you," Sukanya said, but she could not understand what Janaki would demand from her. The aura of the entire family was so impressively etched in the mind of Sukanya that it was Sukanya who was always on the receiving end in front of Janaki.

"Will you be my daughter-in-law?" She had spread out the loose end of her saree that she was wearing in front of Sukanya.

Sukanya felt as if she had heard something wrong. She had lost her mother in her childhood, then lost her father, and then lost her mother-like Amma. She suffered so many misfortunes. However, her life's most excellent fortune was that she was staying under their protection in their house. She had neither imagination nor desire for tremendous wealth than that.

"Daughter, there is no pressure on you, nor we ask you to repay a favour, nor seek your reply with the intent that you have been in this house for so many years, you have been with us more for your virtues and not because of our kindness."

She had always known Ambuj as the owner of this house. The reticent Ambuj had never spoken to her much even before, or even afterward. While Varsha had been alive, there had been no urgency even need to talk to Sukanya, and neither Sukanya had a habit of finding an opportunity to speak.

After the demise of Varsha, occasionally, he would talk to Sukanya regarding the progress of his daughters. When Ambuj returned home after Poonam's episode, he expressed his gratitude to her visibly through his eyes without saying anything. What had been there in those sad and lonely eyes that she was shaken from inside?

Then Janaki's question? Was God giving a new direction to her fortune? Trishna and Tuhina's face turned around in front of her eyes, and so did Ambuj's.

The social level of Poonam and Sukanya was almost the same and Ambuj's family, in comparison to theirs, was magnificent like the sun shining in the sky. Unfortunate Poonam had tried to grasp her fortune with her jealousy and stubbornness, but she cut a sorry figure by burning her hand. On the other hand, the same sun-charged sphere was eager to spread the moon's coolness over gentle and contented natured Sukanya.

Sukanya wholeheartedly accepted the good fortune as a blessing of God and touched Janaki's feet in gratitude.